Anthony McDonald

GAY ROMANCE ON GARDA

ANTHONY MCDONALD

Anchor Mill Publishing

Gay Romance on Garda

Cover image: August Blue - Henry Scott Tuke

Anchor Mill Publishing

4/04 Anchor Mill

Paisley PA1 1JR

SCOTLAND

anchormillpublishing@gmail.com

Anthony McDonald

For Roger McGeachin

Gay Romance on Garda

ONE

It hadn't crossed my mind that he might be \ ....ui. I'd
prepared myself for almost everything, except that.

I had brought English books with me, and films on
DVD. I'd enquired about dictionaries. They'd said don't
bother. They had Italian / English and the OED.   That
left my luggage the lighter by two door-stops, about
which I was quite relieved. I put in an extra pair of
shorts – and sun-cream: I'd heard that was more
expensive in Italy.

I was also prepared for their house to be amazing. I
knew they were vastly richer than anyone I knew. And
their house certainly was amazing. More about that in a
bit.

Even the arrival had been amazing. Every moment of
it. My plane had skimmed like a sickle-winged bird
across the lake. The peninsula of Sirmione, darting out
from the southern shore into the middle of it, looked like
the tongue of a chameleon. Then we'd banked sharply
and turned back a little way to line up for the runway at
Valerio Catullo.

I was met by a chauffeur. I'll write that again. I was
met by a chauffeur. It had never happened before. We
drove up between pencil-sharp cypress trees to the
house's front door, while the lake winked enticingly at us
from below, between the cypress trunks.

The parents met me in the hall. They were dressed in
that smart-casual way that wealthy Italians have. Which
meant: not particularly casual, but very very smart. I was
glad I'd had the forethought to travel in neatly pressed

chinos rather than in my habitual ripped, knee-revealing jeans. The mother, Signora Luccini, called out in the airy space – for it seemed that all the house's doors and windows were open – for her son to present himself as well. 'Sandro.'

And there he was at once. Materialising from one of the wide-open, sun-streaming doors. And he took my breath away.

He had shiny black hair, which was wavy and quite long. Large brown eyes. Full lips. His small stature, slender build and long hair gave him, for that moment, almost the appearance of a girl. Yet there was an assured masculinity about him also. He was very much a boy. A boy who'd just turned eighteen. Three years younger than I, who had just turned twenty-one, but who was also still very much a boy.

I had just finished university. I didn't know what I wanted to do. Jobs were in short supply anyway. For the next couple of months though, my path was mapped out. I was going to help young Alessandro polish his English – between his leaving school and embarking on a full-time course studying the subject in Rome. Signor Luccini was a business associate of my father's. I'd never have got such a plum job for the summer otherwise.

The chauffeur, who was also a sort of butler, carried my case upstairs to my room. (I won't go on writing twice every sentence that refers to the chauffeur or we'll never get through the book. I think you've already taken my point.)

My room was high-ceilinged, and big enough to dance in. It was furnished with bed, dressing table, wardrobe and chest of drawers that were all swishy curves. They were of walnut and mahogany, I think. I wasn't expert enough to date them. They hadn't been made yesterday, though. I did know that.

But the furniture, even the big bed, drew from me just a quick glance. It was the window that beckoned me. High and wide, it opened to the south west and seemed to be flooded with the lake. Un-obscured by trees from this vantage-point the lake danced its sparkling way from one end of the window-frame to the other. Only the Luccinis' green lawns, sloping down and vertically framed by cypress trees, separated me from its near edge. Far across it the opposite shore ran darkly beneath the incoming sun. How many miles was it across? I didn't know. I would find out. It looked a lot.

Headlands and little mountain peaks punctuated that far skyline. What they were called I had no idea. Again, I would find out. Somewhere out there I was looking at the wooded peninsula of Sirmione. Difficult to tell from here where it began and ended. I heard my breath come out almost like a sigh. I realised that surprise and wonder had trapped it inside me for half a minute or more.

*

There was a cocktail before dinner. I can't tell you what it was. There was sweet Martini in it, I think, and a lot of other things besides. Ice, and a slice of orange, were easier to identify. We drank it in a room from which French windows opened wide onto the lawns. And if my room was beautifully furnished, then this one topped it by a multiple of ten. Pictures of landscapes, and some abstracts, hung on the walls. Wonderful blue and white vases stood on plinths in recesses in the walls... I won't go on. My eye was captured particularly by a grand piano, almost concert size, in a rosewood case. I longed to discover its make. But now was not the time. I needed to talk to Sandro.

I didn't attempt Italian with him. Partly because I would be talking English with him throughout our lessons, starting next morning, and I needed to begin as we were going to go on. And partly because my Italian was pretty shambolic and I didn't want to show myself up.

Just as well I didn't try. Sandro's English was pretty fantastic, I thought. He talked fluently about the school exams he'd just done, about what it felt like to be no longer a schoolboy, about his forthcoming move to Rome. My heart sank rather as I wondered what I would be able to offer him by way of improvement. English swear words perhaps? Vocabulary of interesting and unusual sexual practices? A young woman appeared in the doorway. It was time to go and eat.

There were just the four of us at the big table in the dining-room. I sat opposite Sandro and tried not to gaze into his eyes too longingly or for too long. We ate fettuccini pasta with smoked trout and artichoke hearts. A breaded veal cutlet with a green salad full of herbs. Then fresh raspberries and cream. A moderate amount of white wine.

I learnt two interesting things at dinner. Well, a lot of interesting things actually, but these were the two that seemed to matter most. One was that Sandro would be heading out on his motorbike, as soon as the meal was done, to meet up with his girlfriend. Well, that answered one question that I'd hardly even got around to formulating in my mind. The other was that we would be five at dinner from tomorrow onwards. Sandro's brother would be returning home after a week with a friend in the mountains. Like me he had finished university just a couple of weeks ago. We were the same age, more or less.

Signora Luccini was a good hostess. She let me know that I was welcome to join her husband and herself in front of the TV, or to wander down to the village and get the feel of things, or simply to retire to my room. I chose the second of the three.

*

There was no chance of getting lost on the way to the village. I walked down the terraced lawns to where the garden ended at a wall. There was a gate in the wall, to which I'd been given my own key. It opened onto the pathway that edged the lake, Waves that were no more than ripples slid to within a metre or two of my feet. I turned left, towards the centre of Garda. Its houses clustered invitingly, peering across the water through lakeside trees from around the curve of the little bay. I walked along the beach for a few minutes, until the path became a stone-made promenade, lined with beds of roses on the lake side, while jasmine climbed the land-side walls.

I came to the village a little while after that. Its cafés and open-air bars ran along the waterfront for a good half mile. Each one had its own distinctive patterned sunshades, awnings and chairs.

I walked the whole length of this lake-front welcome. The ways to the village centre lay through arched medieval gates and tempting alleyways. I decided to leave those for another time. Perhaps Sandro would take me on a guided tour of the tucked-away old streets some other day.

One row of tables and chairs, a foot or two from the edge of the lake was set outside a building that looked like the Palace of the Doges in Venice, if on a rather smaller scale. I plumped myself down in one of the chairs and, when the waiter arrived, ordered myself a beer.

Like almost everyone else I sat facing out across the lake. The boats that plied across it carrying tourists all day had stopped for the night, though the water's surface still pulsed with their earlier waves and wakes. The midsummer sun was sinking between two mountains on the far shore. It was causing orange rays like cart-wheel spokes to flare across the sky, and had created a shimmering golden causeway that led all the way from the setting sun to me. For a moment I could imagine myself going on foot across the water, traversing that golden road, until I reached the sun and became one with it. It was one of the most beautiful sights I'd ever seen.

'May I join you?' a voice said.

I looked up, almost jumped up, startled out of my reverie. The voice belonged to a young man, perhaps a couple of years older than me, whose nationality I couldn't at once guess, but about whose looks there was no doubt. He was more than easy on the eye.

'Please do,' I said. 'I'm on my own.' That saved him having to ask later. He sat down next to me.

'What a beautiful sight that is,' my new companion observed. 'I like to sit and watch that every night.' He turned towards me and looked searchingly into my face. 'Are you on holiday here?'

'I'm doing a summer job,' I told him. I thought that was enough to be telling him. At least for now. 'And you?'

'I'm on holiday with my parents,' he said. 'In one of the big hotels. I broke up with my girlfriend a few weeks ago, and they thought it would be good for me to get away.'

'Sorry about that,' I said. 'About the girlfriend, I mean.' But I thought, well, where there's life there's hope. Some guys had reasons for breaking up with girlfriends that were more interesting to me than others. 'Where are you from?' I asked him.

'Austria,' he said. 'And you?'

'England. I'm Henry.'

'Tobias,' said my companion. It sounded like *Two Beers.*

The waiter re-materialised and, as if repeating his own name, Tobias ordered one for himself and, without checking whether I wanted it or not, a second one for me.

I learned something I'd never thought about before. That for landlocked Austria and southern Germany Lake Garda was the coast. They whizzed down to it through the tunnels of the Alps in no time at all. 'But staying here with parents,' Tobias said, 'well, it could be worse... but it could be better.'

My heart went out to him when he said that. It was a little moment of bonding. 'I know what you mean,' I said.

He gave me a look. It's difficult to be sure, when you're dealing with someone of a different nationality, and who speaks a different language, how to interpret things. It's difficult enough even when the other person lives next door. But something in the look that Tobias gave me then told me – I thought – that, ex-girlfriend or no ex-girlfriend, Tobias was gay.

I decided to throw out a little line. Twirling my beer in my glass I said, 'I've come down here to teach English to an eighteen-year-old Italian boy.' I noticed Tobias prick up his ears and eyes at that, although he tried to pretend he hadn't. 'In one of the big houses round the bay.' I gestured nonchalantly towards the wooded hillside across the sweep of water that was now growing silver and charcoal in the dusk. 'I just arrived today.' I saw Tobias nod with an interest he could no longer disguise. I threw out some more line. 'The boy is beautiful,' I said.

'You find boys beautiful,' Tobias said. Almost sighed. Then, very softly, 'So do I.'

I said, 'I think you're rather lovely, Tobias.'

'In which case,' said Tobias wistfully, 'I don't think I have vocabulary enough for you.'

My cock was revving in my chinos by this stage. I had no doubt that the situation inside the jeans Tobias was wearing was much the same. I saw his knee begin to bounce impatiently with those pent-up things we know about but are hard to name.

'Do you have somewhere we can go?' I asked. He was the older one but I worried that, despite his excellent English, he might not have had at his finger-tips the colloquial expression that was required just then. So I had said it for both of us.

Tobias shook his head. He looked pained. Like a schoolboy suddenly. 'The hotel... Where my parents are... It's not possible there.'

'And I'm a guest up there...' I pointed again towards the bay, now pewter and black. 'Alleyways here in the village...?'

'Or walking back towards your place, along the beach,' Tobias suggested seamlessly.

We walked back, the way I had come, occasionally clasping hands. We couldn't see the jasmine now, we couldn't see the roses, but we smelled them as we passed. Roses to the left, between us and the darkly silver water. Jasmine between us and the cypress-scented hillside to our right.

We stopped when there were no lights from the village to shine on us directly. Though we could see them twinkling, copper, a little way away around the bay. Tobias was not only older than I was but bigger. He took command. He very gently backed me against the wall and started kissing me. I let him take charge of the mantelpiece, as it were, while I focused my attention on the fire. He had a complicated belt buckle (don't they always?) but with a little Houdini-like effort I got it undone. I pulled his jeans down and then his briefs. And, blow me, despite his attentions to my lips and the intimate cavity beyond them, within a second he'd got my chinos down.

He had a very big prick, had Tobias. I hadn't recce-ed it before. I'd thought mine was of a reasonable size, but I found myself quite literally – though pleasantly – out-gunned.

I felt around his buttocks. They were round and firm.

He felt mine. I was conscious of his feeling them and, with my mind's fingers, tried to feel them as Tobias was feeling them then, making a mind picture of his experience like the echo-location of a bat.

We both knew this was going to be a quickie. Nothing epic would occur. We started to masturbate each other confidently. Each of us well aware we'd done this many times before. It was an experience both comfortable and comforting.

There was a rustle nearby. We froze. We stood among the shadows of the trees while a couple, one male one female, walked past us, just two feet away. They must have seen us, immobile as two marble statues. Tobias's buttocks, thighs and calves, 'Marble like solid moonlight,' as Chesterton wrote, and my more dimly lit loins and knees. They must have smelled us, musky, brinier than the briny lake, but were kind enough to avert their gazes, make no comment and pass carelessly on. I hoped they loved each other, and had bigger things to concern themselves with than a passing encounter with two horny male strangers on a lakeside beach path in the dark.

'I think I'm going to come,' I said.

'Do it over me,' was Tobias's unequivocal reply. So I shot into his groin and drenched his pubes, and a second later he did the same to me.

We wiped each other down inadequately with paper tissues, then pulled our pants and trousers up.

'Will I see you again?' I asked. Suddenly anxious. Suddenly a little child.

'No,' said Tobias, suddenly the adult now. 'We leave

tomorrow. I don't give you my email address or phone. It's not a good idea.'

'No,' I said, in an adult, manly way. 'You're right.' But inside I was a little boy again, all ready to crumple up and cry. And die.

I made the best of it. I kissed Tobias's cheek, standing a little on tiptoe. 'You were lovely,' I said.

He said, *'Und du.'* I didn't have that much German, but I knew that meant, *So were you.*

He kissed my cheek, then we turned away from each other and parted, in our opposite directions along the lake's night-scented shore.

I fumbled for my key to the garden gate and let myself in. When I knocked diffidently at the front door the chauffeur butler let me imperturbably through. There was no sign that anybody else was still up. I took myself to bed quietly. Earlier I'd imagined I'd have to masturbate myself to sleep with thoughts of Sandro. That was before I'd met Tobias. But I still masturbated, once I got between the sheets, thinking of Sandro. And then, thinking of Tobias, I did it a second time.

TWO

Sandro's bedroom was even bigger and better than mine. Although it was a bit less tidy and neat. But if mine was tidy that was only because I'd been occupying it for a rather shorter time than he'd been using his.

I'd never taught English before. I'd never taught anybody anything before. We sat opposite each other at his computer-cluttered desk. There were Sandro's eyes in front of me, deep pools to drown in, miniature representations of the lake that sparkled and enticed beyond the window pane. My heart was still heaving with the unexpected encounter with Tobias just twelve hours ago. This was all going to be very difficult. I was like the sea on the morning after a storm.

'Your English is very good indeed,' I began by saying to Sandro. He rewarded me with a lovely smile. 'We must find ways to develop it further. In the directions that you want it to go.' I was pleased with the sound of this. What I meant by it I had no idea.

'But I thought we'd begin,' I went on, 'by just checking a few basic things.' From my briefcase I pulled with a flourish the complete list of English irregular verbs. It was pretty long, and I thought it would get us through quite a big chunk of the morning, giving me time to think what on earth I could possibly do next. It was the list that includes verbs like *beget, begat, begotten*, and *shrive, shrove, shriven*. Verbs that haven't been used since the King James Bible was written four hundred years ago. Knowledge as useful for anyone going to work in today's world as knowing how to thresh corn with a flail.

Sandro ran his eyes down the list. 'This is all of them,' he said, in a tone of surprise. 'At school we always used the shorter list. You know, the seventy or so that we use every day.'

'It doesn't hurt to know the others,' I said, bluffing. I'd reckoned without the fact that Sandro had spent ten years being taught English at his school by people who knew what they were doing – unlike me.

So we spent the next hour and a half reading through this massive list of words, and testing each other on chunks of it. After a time it seemed to become a kind of Doomsday project. It felt as if we were trying to memorise the bible itself. I saw Sandro's face transform itself gradually from resigned acceptance of an unwelcome task towards something approaching a sulk. His lower lip drooped and trembled at times.

By the time we stopped for coffee my head was swimming with useless verbs: *smite, smote, smitten; geld, gelt, gelt...* I found myself having to take deep breaths so as not to faint. So what state Sandro's head was in I hardly dared imagine. Like scrambled egg, most probably, with a little silent fury stirred into it in place of salt.

I'd wanted to make a friend of Sandro. But I realised that in the course of half a morning I was on the way to turning him into an enemy for life. It was his mother who saved the day. She had coffee with us and, reading the situation in both our faces, not needing to ask, offered us the escape route we needed. Offered us the salvation, for both of us, from myself.

'You should go out, you boys,' she said. 'Enjoy the

17

summer while you can.' She turned to me. 'The whole world is a classroom. And everything in it has an English name. There are a lot of those that Sandro won't know. There is everything in the world out there to talk about, without even going further than the shore of the lake.'

*

We went just a little further than the shore of the lake. We set out across its glittering surface in a boat. I taught Sandro the words *outboard motor, tiller, and pull-cord.* He taught me how to start the engine, use the throttle, and steer.

The smile came back into Sandro's face. The light shone again in his eyes. Sunlit ripples on the lake were reflected in little waves of light that swam across the soft skin beneath his chin and nose. We talked about everything under the morning sun. Our moribund English course had magically come alive.

*

We forgot to go home for lunch. We were enjoying each other's company so much. Sandro talked readily. Just occasionally he'd make a small mistake. I'd think about it a moment, then we'd talk about it, explore its hinterland. And so little lessons were born naturally, arising from things we talked about, and things we did and saw. It reminded me of when I'd learned to ride a bicycle. Suddenly I was teaching English, without quite knowing how. I was learning how to teach.

But you can only forget about lunch for a couple of hours or so. We powered our way shoreward and into the miniature harbour that extended out from the promenade where I'd sat last night – and had had my two beers with Tobias.

The village shared its name with the lake on whose shore it had been founded centuries before. Garda was the lake, Garda the village too. It was set in a west facing bay, sheltered from the north wind by a massive spur of rock: the long headland that Sandro's family home was built on; it ran on westward a couple more miles to the Punta San Vigilio. Looking back from the harbour wall after we'd tied up and got out of the boat, we could see the Luccinis' house, bathed in sunshine, above its lawns and through its cypress trees, on the side of the hill. Beyond it the Punta San Vigilio stretched out, like a crocodile half-submerged in water, with yet more cypress trees forming a crest along its scaly back, and all the way to the tip of its nose.

Sandro seemed to pick a café at random. Though when we'd sat down under the row of sunshades outside, he greeted the waiter by name as he arrived. I wondered if he knew all the waiters in all the cafés along the waterfront, and thought that he probably did.

The disappointing thought was that he probably knew the names of all the waitresses too. After several hours of non-stop conversation I'd had to draw the conclusion that he was heterosexual through and through. He told me about his girlfriend Daniela. She too came from a wealthy local family. They lived a little further up the hill. They'd been at school together. Now university beckoned them both. But she was going to Padua, he to Rome. He made a little moue.

We had a bright gold beer that sparkled in the sun. That cheered him, after his momentary dip into thoughts of that imminent parting. And we ate a bruschetta – tomatoes, olive oil, garlic and herbs, on crusty toast. That would keep us going for the few hours that remained till dinner time. Meanwhile I taught Sandro the expression, *tie up* a boat. He seemed delighted with it, having until then known only the verb *to moor*. The uses of *tie up* were legion, I discovered, as we explored the subject together then. I didn't have a girlfriend to talk about, which was slightly uncomfortable, so *tie up* had to do instead. To my surprise it kept us going happily for a good while.

'Did you come down here last night?' Sandro asked me at one point. I hadn't asked him where he'd gone, or what he'd done, with his girlfriend the previous evening. When it's a couple you obviously don't. It's different when someone's on their own.

'Yes,' I said. 'I sat outside a café a bit further down.' I gestured in the direction. 'The one that looks like the Doge's Palace. I got talking to a guy from Austria.'

'An Ostrich.'

'No, that's a bird. You say, an Austrian. He was called Tobias.' Somehow I found it was important that I spoke his name.

'Two Beers?' queried Sandro and giggled.

I spelt it for him. 'On holiday with his parents,' I said, though to Sandro this couldn't have mattered less. 'He'd split with his girlfriend.'

'That's a bummer,' said Sandro, who was picking up my vocabulary fast. I itched to tell him how we'd gone on and had sex by the wall on the way back to Sandro's parents' house. I couldn't, of course. Perhaps when I knew him better, though...

*

I was quite warm and red-skinned by the time we got back to the house. I'd been bombarded by the sun's rays all day, not just pouring out of the sky but reflected back off the huge expanse of water that was Garda lake. I had a shower. There was still some time before dinner.

Somerset Maugham wrote that the space between tea-time and the cocktail hour is the most difficult part of the day to fill. What a different world he lived in! And yet I have to say I find that to be one of the deeper truths. Sandro was sitting in the garden when I came down from the shower, just staring out across the lake. I knew he'd talked enough for now, and needed some time to chill, re-setting his thought-mode to Italian. I asked him if anyone would mind if I played the piano for a bit. He said, 'Go ahead.'

Everybody who plays the piano even moderately well knows the feeling of lifting the fall-board of a nice looking instrument in someone's house, only to discover, as they start to play, that it's out of tune, the touch is lumpy and uneven, and some of the keys stick or else, when depressed, produce no sound beyond a wooden knock. They know the experience of then valiantly trying to play a phrase or two, so as not to disappoint their hosts, before abandoning the attempt with a brave smile.

So it was with apprehension that I opened the instrument up. But the name on the inside of the fall-board stopped me in my tracks. Fazioli. The greatest Italian make of modern times. One of the finest instruments, these days, in the whole world.

I dared to get my hopes up. I sat down. I thought I could just about remember Bach's first keyboard partita in B flat. I took a breath and launched myself.

I could hardly believe it. It was like the piano was playing the piece to me, not I playing the piece on it. Every nuance of thought I had, conscious or unconscious, about how it should sound from note to note, was picked up, it seemed, by the instrument, and interpreted for my benefit. It was as if the instrument were saying to me, 'Listen. This is how it should go...'

I played through the first movement of the partita; the rather prim, peremptory little prelude that lasts about a minute and a half. Encouraged – no, more than encouraged, I was almost overwhelmed – I dived straight into the next section, the let-your-hair-down Allemande. Officially a courtly dance it comes over – and it certainly did now – more like a headlong chase through fields and woods. I thought of myself in pursuit of Sandro. The piano picked up the idea and together we ran with it till the piece came to a stop. On a falling chord. As if, after running, you were stooping and spreading your hands down the front of your thighs as you caught your breath.

I was aware that people had come into the room and had sat down, and were listening attentively. I didn't look up to greet them or to see who they were. That would have been a fatal mistake. I was conscious, though, that in the half second's pause between the Allemande and the fiery, prancing Corrente that follows it, cantering and capering like a colt, I could have heard a pin drop.

I played the whole thing. The slow, elaborate Sarabande that fanned out its display of harmonic colours like a peacock's tail, the two little minuets, and then the final jig, romping around the keyboard, the two hands leap-frogging each other in fast motion towards the whirlwind finish. It seemed to pass in a second.

The partita was ended. I looked round. The room seemed full of people. None of them clapped. Instead they all wore radiant smiles. It was like the sun was shining from their faces. It was better than applause.

There, scattered like cushions around the chairs and sofas, sat Signor Luccini and his wife. There was Sandro, grinning from ear to ear. The chauffeur butler. The young woman who worked in the kitchen and elsewhere, doubling up as secretary and cook.

And in addition to that lot, sitting in an armchair a little way apart, there was the most beautiful apparition I'd seen in my entire life.

He didn't look at all like Sandro. Sandro had his father's dark, Italian skin and eyes. His brother – for this could only be he, though he was nearly twice as big – had his mother's fairer complexion. He was of the Lombard type. Flaxen hair, chocolate brown eyebrows, lashes and beard... Yes, he had a beard. It was trimmed very close, though, almost to the condition of stubble, so it didn't hide his sculpted face. His eyes were very light blue, and his skin, which was visible even in the stubbly bearded part, was the colour of honey ice-cream, with a light strawberry flush to the cheeks.

I knew from that first moment that I wanted him.

Everyone began to stand up. Some clapped. All spoke. In Italian, of course. I couldn't pick out the words, with everyone talking to me at once. But I got the gist. I was wonderful. They'd had no idea I could play. That I could play like that... I was a wonderful surprise, a find. A lovely addition to the family for the summer.... Well, I *think* that's what was said.

Michele... I had to dredge the name out of my memories of yesterday's conversations – the name had meant nothing to me at the time – Michele alone hung back. He stood, but remained on the far side of the room, near the chair he'd been sitting in. Perhaps he hadn't appreciated the music as much as the others had. Perhaps he wasn't musical. Not everyone likes Bach. And anyway, I wasn't really all that good...

Then he walked towards me, slowly, but ignoring the others in his path. He was an inch taller than I am. (I'm six foot.) He came right up to me, and shone his blue eyes into the hidden places of my eyes and heart. 'Henry,' he said. He wasn't smiling, though.

Henry is easy to pronounce. Michele perhaps not. His wasn't a French girl's name, but that of an Italian boy. It goes Me-kay-lay, with the accent on the kay. Right, we've sorted that. 'Michele,' I said.

'Can you play something else?' he asked in English. Faultless. With hardly a trace of Italian accent.

'Do you like Mozart?' I asked him.

'Yes please,' he said. And then he did smile. And to my utter amazement I saw that his eyes were filling up.

THREE

We sat next to each other at dinner. How else would we sit? But we were tongue-tied now. We both knew that a great wave had engulfed the pair of us, though we didn't know its nature yet. We had everything to talk about, we knew that also, but we couldn't begin just yet.

I'd played the first movement of a Mozart sonata, in response to Michele's request. The others had all stayed to listen. At the end of the movement I stood up, to signal that the mini-recital was over, Everyone said thank you again, and how gorgeous, and dispersed. It was cocktail time. But I didn't move far from the piano, and Michele moved towards me again. He said, 'Play the other two movements, just for me,' as I already knew he would. So I sat down again and did so. Just as he'd known I would.

We had penne pasta with asparagus and pesto, the whole dish a brilliant spring-like green. Then wild salmon with summer spinach. And finished with a frothy, creamy lemon thing, chilled in ornate glasses. It was something between a syllabub and a mousse, I thought.

There was a difficult question I had to put to Michele. It may not be the one you're thinking of. I asked him, 'Are you also a pianist?'

He said, 'I play the piano, yes. Though not as well as you. But I do sing.'

That could have meant anything. I said, 'What sort of stuff?'

'Oh, just the usual. Operatic arias. Verdi, Puccini, Mozart...' Just the usual... I was forgetting we were in Italy. 'And German Lieder, too. Schubert...' He grimaced. 'My German accent's not great. I like Reynaldo Hahn's songs also. French is easier for me. And you?' Charitably perhaps, he said, 'I guess you do all that too.'

I nearly choked on my penne and asparagus. Me? Sing all that stuff? I'd been known to deliver the odd Beatles' song at parties if someone else knew the chords for guitar. But the thought of me belting out Verdi, or teasing out the vocal subtleties of Reynaldo Hahn... 'No. No way,' I said.

I took the next bull by the horns. 'Are you professional?'

He rocked his head from side to side, not shaking, twisting it, in the usual gesture that means no, but inclining it first left, then right. It was a gesture I'd never before seen anyone make. I thought it was sweet. I thought it was more than that.

'I'd like to be,' he said. 'But there's thousands of us in Italy who'd like to be. And that's just tenors. Add in the baritones and basses...' He shook his head, in the more usual fashion this time.

Then he flushed slightly, in the way of people whose manners are impeccable, when they apprehend some tiny fall from their own grace. 'But sorry. I mean, what about you?'

'No, no. No way,' I said. But then I added, because I was a little bit proud of the fact, 'My mother trained as a concert pianist. I guess a little may have rubbed off.'

Sandro brought us down from our lofty heights with a healthy shot of irreverence. 'Hey, 'Chele,' he called to his brother across the table, 'Signor Henry made a friend last night, who's called Two Beers. What are the chances of that?'

Michele turned to me, wearing a puzzled grin. 'Explanation?' he asked.

I explained the Tobias, two beers thing. 'Where did you meet him?' Michele asked. He made it sound the most casual of questions, or line of questions. I knew very well that it was not.

'Outside one of the bars along the waterfront.' I knew the name of the building by now. 'The Loggia della Losa.' Built in the fifteenth century. I'd also learned that.

Again as if it were the least important of things Michele asked me, 'Seeing him again tonight?'

'He went back home to Austria this morning,' I said in a neutral voice. Also as if this were a matter of no earthly consequence. And then I shut my mouth and waited. Michele was on his home turf, I was the stranger. The next move was his.

Until he made it I counted the seconds. There were four of them. They were long ones, I'll admit. And then he said it. Quite simple and straight out. 'Do you want to go down there with me tonight?'

With all my heart.

I said, 'Hey, yeah. Be nice, that would.'

I could so easily have pressed my knee against his

beneath the table top. He could have done the same. I was conscious that it would have required only a movement of an inch or so by either of us. But neither of us did. I think all kinds of different things – the places we were, Italy, his parents' house, the dinner table – kept us in check.

I thought how wonderful it was that we had an interest in common. A shared love of the kind of music that most people think of as rather serious, although usually it is not. But that was a bonus really. We had bigger things in common. By now I was fairly certain of that.

*

'We can take my car,' he said, as we went out of the front door and closed it behind us, 'or we can walk.'

I glimpsed the car, parked a little way behind the others on the gravel sweep. It was a Lamborghini Aventador, in burgundy red. I'd never sat inside, let alone driven, anything so wonderful. Until that moment I'd have given my eye-teeth. I said, 'Let's walk.'

We followed the track of my lone footsteps of this time last night. Down the stepped terraces of the lawns, between the cypress trees, to the wall between us and the lake. Arriving at the gate in the wall, I produced my key from my pocket before Michele had time to get hold of his. I did it with a dramatic flourish and he laughed. 'You have your own key, even,' he said. 'That makes you really one of us.'

We opened the gate and stepped through it, and were met by the sight, and smell – briny and edged with summer leafage – of the lake. As we turned left along the rough track through beach and bushes, Michele asked me, 'So this Two-Beers character. How did you meet?'

'I was sitting at a table on my own,' I said. 'He asked if he could join me. Simple as that.'

I longed to tell Michele that we were at that moment passing the spot where Tobias had pressed me gently against the wall and pulled my trousers down, and I'd lowered his. The spot where I'd finally shot my load into his belly hair and his sperm had trickled down the inside of my legs. Where I'd clasped his naked thighs and buttocks – marble like solid moonlight – and a couple had seen us and walked on past. I looked at the place as we went by it, Michele oblivious to its significance, and I felt almost a sense of disbelief that it had happened. There. So recently. It seemed an episode from a previous life.

'The Austrians are famous as heavy drinkers,' Michele remarked. 'Did you both have a lot?'

'Just two beers,' I said.

*

The waiters at the Loggia recognised me from the previous evening. They recognised Michele too, of course. You could see the cogs whirring in their heads, as happens when two people known from different contexts turn up together in the same place. Michele got the drinks order in before I could. He did it in English, to the waiter's surprise. 'Two beers,' he said. Then he shot me a very mischievous smile.

We began to talk. We didn't bother with Do you have a girlfriend? We knew enough by now to realise that even if either of us had had one yesterday, by tomorrow we wouldn't have. It was a matter of complete irrelevance.

Instead Michele said, 'Sandro likes you.'

I said, 'I'm glad of that. Since we're going to spend so much time together.' I paused, undecided whether to say the next thing or not. I decided I would. 'I thought it was all going to go wrong this morning, though,' I confessed. 'I made a stupid mistake...' I was going to tell him the irregular verbs story but he cut me off.

'Yes, Sandro told me before dinner. But you're more than forgiven, apparently. He says you're great company out on a boat...'

I laughed. Michele went on. 'He really likes you now. You're lucky, because he doesn't bestow his affections lightly.' *He doesn't bestow his affections lightly!* Where had Michele got that from? Had he learnt not only Puccini and Verdi off by heart but the classics of English literature as well?

'Do you?' I said. 'Bestow your affections lightly?' I wasn't sure where I was going with that, or why I'd said it. The conversation seemed to be playing itself out of its own accord, without either of us doing very much to control it. It was like something outside of both of us.

'No,' he said. We were sitting side by side, looking out over the lake. At this moment it was an astonishing cobalt blue. The sun hadn't crashed in flames among the mountains yet, though soon it would. We half turned our heads when either of us spoke, just for a second, to catch each other's reaction to what had just been said. And as we exchanged our cautious questions and answers, not giving too much away just yet, we saw each other's facial expressions, and the thoughts behind them, gradually converge, so that they began to mirror each other. I began to see a little bit of myself inside Michele. He began to see something of himself in me.

It was too good to last, I thought. Nothing quite like this had happened at the start of any other relationship I'd had. But it was peaking too soon. It would last the next hour or so only, while we had a couple of drinks. By breakfast tomorrow it would be all over. Something to look back on with a wistful smile, but gone. A brief evening candle that the night had snuffed out.

'Do you have a boyfriend back home?' Michele asked. No adjective or adverb exists to describe the complexity of thought, the multi-layered feelings, that escaped into his tone of voice.

'No,' I said. 'I have had boyfriends. But at the moment, no.' There were long stories behind that answer of mine. I wondered if I would ever find myself sharing them with Michele. 'What about you?'

'Ditto, ditto,' he said softly.

Oh wow. Oh fuck.

I tried to peer downwards at his crotch to see if he showed any sign of an erection, but from the position I sat in I couldn't have seen without half standing up and making it much too obvious what I was trying to do. I could be quite unsubtle, people had told me, but I wasn't as unsubtle as that. I said, 'I sat here last night and watched the sun go down over the mountains and the lake and it all went gold and then the water turned silver and the mountains black and it was one of the most wonderful things I'd seen in my entire life.' I had to stop.

Michele said, 'Take a breath.' I did. 'Was Tobias with you then?' Michele asked. There is a word for the way he asked this. Pretend-casual is the one.

'No,' I answered. 'He arrived after that.'

Michele said, 'Me too, I like to sit here and see the sun go down, It's not so good from the house. It goes behind the trees some minutes before it sets. It's not the same thing.'

Then we sat in silence for a while, watching its descent. At first it seems hardly to move at all, then at the last minute it speeds up. Cartwheels of gold, that momentary causeway across the water, a final chirp of blinding light, then gone, leaving only flames behind the mountains, and a sky the red-gold of the curtain in an opera house.

To my astonishment I felt Michele's hand on my thigh. Not a tentative, exploring nervous finger – I'd been on the receiving end of those, and done it myself, often enough in the past – but a big manly squeeze and grip. Only for a second though. Michele had made his gesture in full view of everyone who was walking past, and there was nothing furtive about the way he withdrew his hand either. He said, 'We're funny in Italy.'

'Why funny?' I asked. 'Funny in what sense?' I made no attempt to reciprocate his contact. He'd done it for both of us.

'Because, unlike men in America and northern

Europe – unlike you – we hug and kiss each other a lot. We're very physical with one another, and it doesn't signify anything more than casual friendship or a moment of high spirits. Except those of us who're gay. And then, the funny thing is, we have a difficulty with that.'

'I can understand that,' I said. 'It's not so very different where I come from, though. It's the same thing in principle. Just a matter of degree. A few days ago I heard two big Rugby players, with their wives, call each other darling in a pub.'

I stopped, embarrassed suddenly. Did I want Michele to call me darling? Not today, perhaps, but one day in the future? Did he too want that? I cast away the wish. It wouldn't happen. This evening was just a brief candle of a moment, I'd already told myself. The night would blow it out.

'Did you get to see his cock?' Michele said. Bloody hell, that came as a shock.

'Whose?' I managed to say.

'Tobias. Wasn't that who we were talking about?'

'Actually yes,' I said. By now I'd had time to compose myself. 'I did more than see it actually. Want to hear about it?'

Michele did.

I told him the story of what we'd done and where we'd done it. I used the slang, vernacular English words like spunk and shoot. I'd glance at him momentarily as I did so, to see if he understood them. It was a trick I'd learned just that day from teaching

Sandro. It seemed that Michele was familiar with the lot.

'And we walked past the spot earlier, and you didn't tell me?' Michele said. It sounded like a mild reproof or complaint.

'Come on,' I said. 'I didn't know you as well then as I do now.'

'I guess that's true,' he said, and sounded mollified.

Both our glasses were empty suddenly. 'Do you want another beer?' I asked him.

'Yes,' he said, to my surprise and perhaps his own. 'I think perhaps I would.

FOUR

We had three beers altogether, actually. By the time we'd finished them it was really dark. Then, as we began our homeward walk, Michele pulled me aside as we crossed the Piazza Catullo, and led me down an alleyway that became a tunnel beneath old houses, to where there was a little piano bar. It was tiny, barrel-vaulted like an old cellar, and packed with people, but Michele shouldered his way to the miniature counter and ordered a nightcap for us both.

It was some sort of fiery spirit. God knows what. I didn't really care. I wasn't quite sure why Michele had brought me here. We were both more interested by now in the idea of sex than more drinking, I had thought. And Michele was, I guessed, like most Italians, not really into heavy drinking anyway. Perhaps he was nervous about what was going to happen next – I knew I was – and was simply delaying the moment when we would have to find out. But it also crossed my mind that, in his home village, a place where it would have been difficult for a gay guy of his age and social standing to be open about his sexuality, Michele actually wanted to show me off. If so, that was quixotic and brave of him. He was risking his cred for me. If that were the case – though I tried not to feel too cocksure about it – then it was one hell of a compliment.

I wasn't introduced to anyone in that scrum. Rather, I saw an an occasional nod of recognition pass between Michele and someone else or other, and a little inclination of the head – almost imperceptible to an onlooker – towards me. I was an outsider here. In

Garda. In Italy too. A new thought struck me. Were there undercurrents, gay undercurrents, flowing here in this lakeside village that I couldn't fathom yet? The thought intrigued me, but I didn't spend long with it. I was more interested in what would happen between Michele and me. What would happen after we left the bar.

I didn't have to wait long to find out. We had just one fire-water nightcap and then left the little cellar, made our way down the tunnel towards the lakeside light at the end of it and turned right along the waterfront towards the house that, in the last couple of hours, I'd come to think of as home.

We walked past the yacht club without saying much, and then, where the village petered out, along the stretch of promenade where there were roses to leftward, lakeside, and jasmine to landward, on our right. You saw them only dimly by the light of the occasional street-lamp, but there was nothing dim about their scent. I felt Michele's fingers reach matter-of-factly for mine at this point. I clasped his equally mattter-of-factly and we walked on hand-in-hand. I was pretty sure that touchy-feely heterosexual Italian males did not do this, however much they might hug and kiss.

I knew we'd stop at the point where I'd had my fun with Tobias the previous night. Michele knew it too. He stopped first. He said, 'I need to piss.'

'Me too,' I said.

He unzipped his jeans quite casually, half facing me, and got his cock out. It was flaccid but long, even so. Uncircumcised. It looked the colour of ivory in the half-light. He didn't bother to pull the skin back as he let his water tumble out. I followed his example in every detail, even if my dick wasn't quite as long as his.

Then, very carefully, because he didn't want us to wet each other's trousers, he leaned towards me, bending at the waist, and kissed me on the lips.

I returned the compliment, also bending towards him from the waist. Our tongues got involved a little. Just testing to begin with, then more and more, exploring the inside of each other's mouth with energy and delight. I'd never before kissed a guy while both of us were emptying out our bladders nonchalantly beside a public path. There's a first time for everything, I thought. And actually I thought it rather nice.

Some things are inevitable, of course. And one was that, as soon as we'd both stopped peeing, our two dicks were hard and pointing up. I reached for Michele's and clasped it, though having got that far, made no further move on it. And he, after breaking off our lips' and tongues' embraces just long enough to look and check that I'd stopped watering the vegetation, followed suit.

Then, gently, I began to masturbate him, but he stopped me after a few seconds. 'Wait,' he said. 'We can do it properly inside the gate.' So we walked on, our two cocks jutting jauntily out of our flies in front of us as we went. It made us giggle, the idea of the two of us walking along like flashers, although we'd have whipped them back inside our jeans as quick as lightning had anybody appeared on the path ahead of us. We held hands though, all the way to the gate, and no-one appeared in front of us or behind, so, with cocks still poking out of our clothing, we unlocked and went through the gate.

Michele knew the garden better than I did, of course. He was on – literally – his home turf. He led me to a close-mown corner of lawn that was tucked behind a line of bushes and thus invisible from the house. Then he pulled me close against him and started to unbutton my shirt.

It didn't take us long to get each other naked. Then we stepped back to admire our handiwork.

Michele was bigger than me, though only a little, in all departments. He had a broad smooth chest, beautiful, muscular, arms and legs and, as already hinted at, a fine up-standing dick. I looked down at my own, equally upstanding but inch-shorter number. 'I can't compete with you dick-wise,' I said.

'Dick-wise?' he queried. It was the first time his English hadn't caught up with mine.

'I mean, with regard to the size of your dick. Your cock.'

He nodded. 'Yes,' he said. 'I'm with you. But you needn't worry. I think you have a lovely one. I think you're all lovely. Every part of you. Anyway, your balls are bigger than mine.'

It was kind of him to notice. 'Only a tiny bit,' I said modestly. At that point he slipped himself smoothly into my arms.

Somehow we were on the ground. We rolled on the grass, enjoyed the sensation of our two hard cocks pressed side by side between our bellies. I could feel pre-come there. Mine or his? From both of us? Who cared? It was nice.

He whispered in my ear. 'Do you want to fuck?' He didn't say whether he meant I'd fuck him or he me.

I hesitated a moment. I hadn't come out with condoms, and probably he hadn't either. We hadn't talked about HIV status, and now was hardly the moment to. I said, 'Maybe not the first time?' with a polite question mark in my voice.

'No,' he said, without sounding disappointed or annoyed. 'That's fine. In fact it's good, what you said.'

'Meaning?'

'Meaning you're thinking there will be a second time. I'm thinking the same.' I liked that too.

We pulled away from each other a little. Or rather, one side of us did. We lay like a half-open book, joined at one hip and shoulder but with our opposite shoulders raised off the ground and just far enough apart for us to be able to look at each other's penis as we went to work on it. I had my other arm round Michele's shoulder and he had his round mine. And intermittently we kissed, as we coaxed each other to climax.

I came all too quickly – that was par for the course with me – but had to persevere with Michele. Eventually he moved my hand away, tenderly, not impatiently, and gently finished the job himself. He had a special way of manipulating his foreskin, I noticed. I took careful note of this for the next time. I had shot on my lower chest. Now Michele pulled himself up a little and rolled towards me, landing his load in exactly the same spot, to mingle with mine. I thought this a clever trick and a charming one. Was it something Italian gay men all did? I would ask him some time. Though not now.

I rolled round on top of him, pushing him onto his back. I felt our intimate patch of wetness spreading under the weight of my chest and tummy, like olive oil between two bits of bread. We lay like that a long time, fondling each other's hair and shoulders, occasionally exchanging a kiss, but we didn't speak.

It was a warm night, otherwise we wouldn't have stayed out there, or even started off in the place we did. But even warm nights grow chilly if you're lying naked near a lake. Eventually we picked ourselves up. We brushed the grass stalks off each other – not so much for practical reasons as for the simple pleasure that intimate touching gave us both. And then, a bit reluctantly, we got dressed.

We walked back towards the house, climbing the stepped terraces of lawns among the cypress trees. I felt a moment of dismay suddenly, of disquiet, call it what you like. The feeling that all too often follows first sex with a friend. I began to see how wise Tobias had been when he vetoed an exchange of contact details between us, even though it had hurt me at the time. With Michele no such option existed. He would be at breakfast the next morning. And quite probably at every breakfast that followed it for the next two months. What had been done had been done. We'd have to live with it together, whatever I – or Michele – might feel about it when in the cold light of tomorrow morning we looked back.

Michele must be a mind reader, I thought, when I

heard what he said next. 'Don't worry, Henry. It's going to be OK. We're going to be OK. That was just a beginning. I'm sure of that.'

Well, if he wasn't a mind reader, that could be accounted for by something else. 'How old are you, Michele?' I asked him.

'I'll be twenty-two next month,' he answered. Yes, that was it.

'I just turned twenty-one last month,' I said. That accounted for quite a lot of things. Michele was my senior by ten months.

We entered the house quietly. It was past midnight and clearly time for bed. We climbed the stairs together, though prudently not holding hands. But we kissed when we reached the landing, and that did go on quite a long and by no means prudent time. At last we broke apart. I headed for my bedroom door, and realised only as we got there that Michele's bedroom was next to mine. He didn't ask me in, though, and I didn't ask him in to mine. 'Goodnight, Henry,' he said as he turned the handle. He smiled. 'Sleep well.'

I returned his smile a bit shyly. 'Sleep well yourself,' I said. And then, with the clicks of two adjacent doors, we parted for the night.

*

Breakfast went better than I'd dared to hope. Although any breakfast that includes strawberries on its menu surely can't ever be all that bad. Michele and I behaved easily and casually towards each other, like any two boys who'd been for a drink together the night before but had done nothing else. We sat opposite each other at table, not side by side as we'd done at dinner last night. And just occasionally we exchanged a tiny look of complicity and amusement that none of the others could see.

There arose the question of what I'd do with Sandro today. Of where we might go. It didn't remain a question for long. 'Can we go to Gardone?' Sandro asked me. I had no objection, obviously, especially as I didn't know where Gardone was. I was able to make a guess, though, that getting there would involve a trip across the lake. I looked at Sandro's mother, my eyebrows raised by way of question marks. I was rewarded by a small nod.

'If you get me there,' I said, addressing Sandro, 'and get me back in one piece.'

Michele put his oar in then, to my surprise. 'Can I come too?' he said.

I adopted a mock-stern manner. 'Only if you promise to speak nothing but English to me and Sandro while we're out.' To say I was delighted would have understated things a bit.

Michele had come to breakfast in a pair of quite long khaki shorts. Smart-casual, of course, and neatly pressed. In the brief chance I'd had to look at them before he took his seat I'd thought his legs had looked lovely in them: finely shaped and nicely muscled, with a light covering of fair hairs. Hairs which my fingers as well as my own legs had familiarised themselves with last night. He was wearing slip-on moccasins without socks, which as it happened, so was I. At this moment I felt suddenly the tickle of Michele's bare toe through my jeans against my calf. I tried not to grin too broadly at him as I looked into his face. And a moment later, I slipped off one of my own moccasins, and raised my own bare toes, and rubbed them ticklingly up and down his naked calf. I felt the hairs there bristle with static. I decided that as soon as breakfast was over I too would change into shorts.

Now Michele turned to his little brother. 'Make sure you take a notebook with you and write things down. Even when we're on the water. Even at lunch. I bet you didn't yesterday.'

'It was the first day,' I said, coming to Sandro's defence before he'd had time to speak. I was still trying to make up for the irregular verbs fiasco. There were moments when I thought I'd be trying to do this for the rest of my life.

'He should start as he means to go on,' Michele said, with a smile but sounding quite serious about it. I thought it rather wonderful that Michele was not only going to come with us, but that we seemed to be getting in role for a nice-cop, tough-cop routine with Sandro, and that Michele was volunteering to be the tough one of us two.

FIVE

Gardone was on the other side of the lake, across from us at its widest stretch, and about nine miles away. I wondered for a moment if we would be going there in the little motor launch Sandro and I had been out in yesterday, but quickly learned that wouldn't be the case. We would queue up and buy tickets for the public boat service at the pier in the village.

The service boats criss-crossed the lake through all the daylight hours. We'd seen them yesterday, and been rocked by their stern waves as they passed. The big hydrofoils, going fast, had given us an especially good shaking.

At a more sedate pace travelled the lake's four old workhorses, named after the cities of the region: Trento, Mantova, Verona and Solferino. (Though Solferino was hardly a city, but rather a village where a famous battle had been fought.) Pleasing to the eye with their white paintwork, their bright red lifebelts looked like rows of festive wreaths of flowers. They had open decks at the top, as well as enclosed ones for bad weather days and for voyagers who were afraid of the breeze.

We travelled this morning on the Verona. After climbing on board we made a beeline for the small triangle of deck in the bows, where the forward view made the seats there especially popular. Michele and Sandro knew all this of course. I simply followed where they led.

'You two look like tourists today,' Sandro observed. 'Both in your shorts.' He seemed mildly perplexed by our choice of leg-wear, he was in jeans himself. I didn't attempt to catch Michele's eye. I knew perfectly well that Michele had chosen shorts because he knew I'd fancy him in them. And vice versa, of course.

I said to Sandro, 'If you've got a day's work ahead of you, it helps a lot if you can dress like you're on holiday.' A day's work indeed! That was outrageous of me. What could possibly feel less like a day's work than taking a boat trip in the sunshine, accompanied by two gorgeous boys, one of whom I'd had sex with the previous night, while looking forward to more of the same this evening? Work? I was in paradise. All I had to do was to converse in my own language. Unlike Sandro, armed on his brother's orders with a spiral-bound writing-pad, I didn't even have to take notes.

The boat didn't hang about. The last passengers had barely floundered up the gangplank before we'd cast off and were turning in a tight circle out towards the open water of the lake. The seats were small and close together. After a moment I felt Michele's bare knee pressing against mine. I pressed mine against his. We kept them there, touching in full view of Sandro and everybody else. It looked quite accidental, as if our knees had to park up against each other because there was no room for them anywhere else. Only Michele and I knew the truth. Another boy's warm knee, his bare skin on yours – the deliciousness of that – the teasing, tickling desire, un-fulfillable in a public space, to touch him somewhere else. I felt myself thicken inside my shorts. I looked and saw that the same thing had happened for Michele.

But I was being paid to teach. And besides, I wanted to show off to Michele. Show him what I'd accomplished already with Sandro. 'What's the water doing, Sandro?' I said.

Sitting on the other side of me, but his knee a respectful and respectable inch away from my free one, he answered, 'Doing? In what way doing? Flowing? Waving?'

'OK,' I said. 'Though we don't say that water waves. There are waves on it. I meant, what we talked about yesterday,' I prompted. 'In the sun.'

'Ah.' Sandro smiled triumphantly. 'It sparkles. Like gassy mineral water, and people's eyes in children's books.'

'Well, that's not bad,' said Michele, sounding impressed. He applied a little further pressure to my knee with his.

We were passing their house now, about half a mile off shore. It sat serenely in the sunshine like a cat. The sloping lawns and sentinel cypress trees looked as tempting as a vision of the Garden of Eden.

'How many words can you think of that begin with GL?' I asked. 'Both of you can play.'

The two Italians thought for a while in silence. Michele's brain-work transmitted itself in a little up-down motion of his leg, a little friction against mine. I could happily go on all day like this, I thought.

'Glitter,' said Sandro.

'Gleam,' offered Michele. Between them they got glimmer and glow, which I thought pretty good going. I gave them glisten and glint.

'And what have they all in common?' I asked.

After a moment's reflection Sandro said, 'They're all about light.'

'Well done,' I said. 'But they're not all interchangeable. The ones with light bright vowel sounds – I and E – are usually about white, brilliant light. The darker vowels, like in glow, usually mean a duller light. More red.'

'So what glitters and what glimmers, then?' Michele asked.

'Diamonds...?' I prompted.

'Diamonds glitter,' said Sandro, 'or sparkle like the waves.'

I could have hugged him. I just said, 'Very good.'

'And glimmer?' Michele asked again.

'Remember coming out of that bar in the tunnel last night?' I suggested without thinking. 'And looking down it to the dim light of the quayside in the distance? Well, that was a glimmer of light, if you like. We also talk about a glimmer of hope.'

'Which reminds me,' Sandro said. 'I meant to ask you – what did you two do last night? It was after midnight when you came back.'

I felt Michele move his knee apart from mine. The question had clearly flustered him. But he hid the fact from his brother well. 'I could ask you what you got up to with Daniela last night, but I won't.'

'No you could not,' Sandro riposted. 'I asked the

question first.'

I answered for Michele. 'We had a beer at the Loggia della Losa, then a nightcap – if you know what that means – at the little piano bar behind Piazza Catullo. Then we walked back along the beach.'

'Back along the beach,' echoed Sandro. Then, in a tone that was more knowing than I felt comfortable with, 'In the dark.' Then I saw him quite distinctly glance down at my crotch, then beyond it to his brother's. It was plain as a pikestaff to anyone who might bother to look there that Michele and I were both half stiff. And it was also as clear as the most glittering, sparkling crystal that Sandro now knew everything there was to know. 'I see,' he said, and gave a little laugh, half of amusement, half of surprise.

Neither Michele nor I could think of anything to say at that point, and so there was silence for a bit. Then Sandro broke it. 'Glamour,' he said.

'Glamour?' I queried.

'It begins with GL,' he said. 'If we're still playing. Is that about light?'

I thought for a moment. 'I suppose it sort of is,' I said. 'Glossy magazines,' I said, off the top of my head. 'They reflect the light.'

'Glabrous,' said Michele suddenly.

'Glabrous?' I said. 'Whatever's that?'

'Smooth, hairless,' Michele answered. Had he swallowed a dictionary when he was a small boy? 'Like a nectarine rather than a peach. Like a baby's bottom.' He mouthed at me, *Or yours.* 'Or like a bald man's head.'

'I suppose that does reflect the light,' I offered, uncertain but hopeful that I'd got this right.

We had reached the Punta del Vigilio, were rounding its tip, turning slightly to the right, a fraction north. I could see now what had been invisible from Garda village, a hotel built of golden coloured stone, that looked like a small palace, and which occupied the extreme tip of the Punta. 'Smart place,' I said, pointing to it.

'And not cheap,' Michele said. 'Prince Charles stays there when he's in the area.'

Sandro said nothing, but he nodded his head. If the Luccini brothers thought the place expensive then it certainly was.

Beyond the Punta San Vigilio we were in sight of the whole long, narrowing, northern reach of the lake. An invigorating breeze was blowing down it: the wind from which the village of Garda's backdrop of craggy rock protected it. It blew all the way from the Alps, from Switzerland. As if to prove the fact, there were mountains in the far distance, beyond the northern limit of the lake, whose peaks were crowned with white. My knee once again sought Michele's, and he willingly pressed back with his own. For comfort, for warmth.

'Who were the silly boys who came dressed in only shorts?' Sandro teased us.

'It'll be hot when we get to Gardone,' Michele told him. 'As you well know. And then you'll wish you'd worn shorts too.'

I certainly found myself wishing Sandro had worn shorts too. You can't have too much of some good things. My erection had gone down now, assailed by the chilly northern blast. So too had Michele's, I noticed. But if it was going to be warm when we got to Gardone, then with any luck, I caught myself thinking, they might pop back up. Without making it too obvious, I rubbed my knee up and down against Michele's leg.

*

We explored *glare*, and *glimpse* and *glassy* as all around us the sunlight glanced off the lake's wavelets, and the opposite shore grew nearer almost imperceptibly.

The other shore. A flat band beyond the water's straight edge. That's all it is at first. But how it changes as you draw near. The band breaks apart into fragments. You are cruising past an island that you didn't know was there. There is a ruined building on it – at least it looks ruined from here. Surrounding it are enchanted gardens, full of trees and climbing flowers. A Sleeping Beauty's castle of an island. You stare at it a long time across the dancing water, then suddenly you have passed it and it's gone. A deep inlet opens up ahead of you where you never imagined one existed. A lakeside town appears around a corner, then is swallowed up by a tree-grown outcrop as your boat sails serenely on. There is nothing quite like approaching a destination over water.

Gardone appeared and took shape in front of us. Church towers and a line of hotels with gardens on the waterfront. Mooring posts like barbers' poles, Venetian style. We tied up. We had arrived.

But that's the trouble with boat trips. The travelling hopefully part is the best. Once disembarked we walked up the waterfront a little way, and then came back. We looked in the windows of shops that sold eye-wateringly priced clothes. I hadn't really seen the shops in Garda village yet, but Michele and Sandro assured me they were much the same as here. We chatted amicably as we walked, Sandro stopping occasionally – bless him – to make a note of a new expression or word. And there was I, desperately wanting to grab hold of Michele and hug him, smother him with kisses, but knowing that in this place I couldn't. It was a longing I felt with my skin's every nerve-ending. It physically hurt.

I wanted to tell Michele this but I couldn't even do that. Though he apparently could. He leaned towards me as we turned a street corner and whispered in my ear, 'I'd like to put my hand up inside your shorts and feel your dick.'

'What are you two whimpering about?' Sandro asked, then mischievously added, 'I don't think you're allowed to whimper in an English class.'

'It's actually whisper, not whimper, I said.' Though Sandro's erroneous choice of word had accidentally come pretty near the mark.

'It was just a private thing,' said Michele. 'Nothing at all.'

'I do know, you know,' said Sandro. He grinned impishly.

I knew that Sandro knew. I knew he'd clocked us when, on the boat, he'd glanced at our two crotches and observed our half hard dicks. I wasn't sure if Michele was aware of this. I hadn't had a chance to ask him yet.

'Know what?' Michele challenged his little brother, though in a teasing voice.

'About you two,' Sandro said.

This could have gone on for some time in the traditional way. *Know what about you two? You know what I mean. No, what do you mean? Etc.* But it didn't. All three of us, I think, were happy to let it go at that.

We returned to the waterside again, in search of a pizza and an ice-cold beer.

I wanted to ask Michele how much Sandro knew about his gayness. I knew it wasn't an easy thing in Italy. I could imagine Michele, as the elder son of a well-to-do family, having difficulty with it. I could imagine his mother and, especially, his father, having difficulty with it. Even if Sandro – to guess from his teasing nibble at the subject – appeared to take it in his stride.

The ride back by the afternoon boat – the Mantova, this time – was as magical as the morning ride across. It was like the replay of a beautiful dream, but on rewind. Again Michele and I sat knee against naked knee. I looked, though not too obviously, at Michele's crotch from time to time and once or twice saw something stir. Then, halfway across the lake I realised there was a little spot of wetness on Michele's shorts, about the size of a large coin. Checking myself with a downward glance I saw the same thing had happened to me.

It didn't escape Sandro's notice either. 'Hey! You two! Bad boys! Look at you both. Big boys like you! You should hope the sun dries you before Momma sees.'

Michele and I had no answer to that, either in English or Italian. We made do with sheepish grins.

The Punta de San Vigilio appeared and then grew large ahead of us; the line of pennants that stood in front of its grand hotel streamed out in the stiff north breeze. Then we rounded it and lost the breeze, while the village of Garda appeared from behind the headland, shimmering in the heat-haze across its sun-trap bay.

It occurred to me that for Michele's dew-drop to have made such a visible impact on his shorts, he must be going commando today. He'd got dressed this morning, I guessed now, without putting on underwear. Well, so had I. He'd done that for me. I'd done it for him. Touché, signor.

SIX

'Could you do something for me when we get back?' Michele asked. We were walking back along the shore, the three of us, away from the jetty where we'd got off the boat.

'Of course,' I answered. I'd have done pretty well anything for Michele by now. But I didn't expect this request to be anything too out of the ordinary, nor anything of a sexual nature. Sandro was padding along beside us after all and was a party to everything that was said.

'Would you play a Schubert song for me? With me,' I mean.

'Yes,' I said. 'If you have the music. I don't know any Schubert accompaniments by heart.'

'I have the music,' he said.

He also had the heart.

We did the first three songs from Die Schöne Müllerin. They went so well, and we worked as such a good team that we then did the last three. The three great ones. Michele had a lovely voice. I'd rather guessed that would be the case. It sounded light and boyish in the first three songs, which he took pretty fast. Then, in the last three, so heart-melting and poignant, he slowed the tempo, found grandeur and a simple beauty. He did them all in German and, though he'd said his accent in that language wasn't very good, it sounded perfect to my ears.

The flowers you gave me shall lie in my grave. But when you wander that hillside, they'll bloom again.

Then May is come and winter gone. In case you don't know the story, the spurned narrator is about to leap to his death in the mill-pond at this point. *When love struggles free from pain at last, a little star, a new one, shines from the sky.* The last words of the last song are the mill-stream's voice. *Good night, then, good night, till the day when all shall wake... Sleep out thy sorrow, sleep out thy joy. The mist is vanishing, the full moon shines; vast heaven above is opening wide.*

The word love had not been mentioned between Michele and me. Why should it be? We'd known each other only twenty-four hours. But here it was now in German. Safely encrypted in a song and someone else's words. Yet, despite the fact that the others came into the room during the time that Michele sang and I sight-read, I knew that Michele was singing for me alone. For me, and to me. Though he didn't dare point the words too obviously or too often in my direction he did so occasionally, and they pierced my heart.

When we'd finished, the others trooped out, saying nice things as they went. Michele's mother stayed a few seconds longer, sitting, giving Michele, then me a look that I can't describe. When two people who love each other make music together a sensitive listener picks up more than mere music, mere words. I think that Signora Luccini had heard, seen, felt something that spoke more eloquently about what was happening to her elder son and me, and told of deeper secrets, than a mere damp patch on two pairs of shorts.

*

Not until after dinner were Michele and I alone. We took the car this time. The Aventador, in which I'd been longing to ride. We drove down the lake to

Lazise, two villages away, south along the shore. The initial acceleration as Michele spurted off pushed me back in my seat as if I'd been in a fighter plane. I did now what I'd longed to do all day: I ran my hand up Michele's warm bare leg and into his shorts. But our journey was fast and brief. I barely had time to reach his happily accessible cock before it was time to withdraw my hand for the sake of public decency. For we had arrived outside the ancient walls of Lazise and were parking up outside the town's great gate.

I said, as we got out of the car, 'There's so many things I've wanted to say all day. But now … I don't know where to start.'

'It's the same for me,' he said. 'But we've got all evening. Let's just walk a bit. We've got all night.'

All this night. And then the next one. But how many after that? My mind shied away from that difficult thought.

Inside the gate we turned into an alley that took a crooked route between walls from which valerian sprouted in red-flowering tufts. Humming-bird moths hovered and darted, thrusting their tongues, which were as long as the rest of them, into flower after red flower. Say the easy bit first, I thought. 'You sing wonderfully,' I said. 'I nearly had to stop playing twice. You nearly made me cry.'

'Thank you. You were a wonderful accompanist.' Then his voice shifted a gear. It was as though he didn't mean to say the next thing that came out, but couldn't help himself. 'Oh Christ, you're beautiful.'

'Oh fuck, Michele. So are you.'

We couldn't hug, we couldn't kiss. There were people coming round the corner ahead of us. I wanted us to be in bed, or lying out under the stars together on the lawn. But that was still a few hours off; the sun hadn't left the sky.

The people passed behind us and for a second we threw caution away, or it abandoned us. We were in each other's arms, kissing lips, our hips thrust forward, cock against cock through shorts. It was just for a second, though. We had to pull apart.

I became practical. 'How much does Sandro know?'

'Well, he knows about us, obviously.'

'He saw our cocks in our shorts on the boat this morning. I saw him clock them. They gave us away.'

Us. I loved the idea that Michele had used that word. First time. And now I'd used it too.

'He's known that I'm gay for some time,' Michele said. 'Guessed, anyway. Though we've never discussed it. Today was as near as he's ever got to talking about it.'

'How did he find out? You don't show any obvious signs...' I was fishing naughtily. I knew that. So did he, but I felt he didn't mind. I wanted to find out all about him. Previous boyfriends. His sex life up to now. I knew that he was itching to find out those same things about me.

'Sandro knows that when I had girlfriends in the past I never went to bed with them. He and I are very close. He used to ask me, and I'd say no. He wanted to learn from his big brother, I think, so from that point of view

I was a disappointment to him. Also it was a bit unusual, these days even in Italy, to have a girlfriend and not have sex with her. Anyway, Sandro didn't seem to need much tuition. He's been screwing like a rabbit since he was fourteen.'

'And you?' I had to ask. 'Have you been screwing boys like a homosexual rabbit since you were fourteen?'

He laughed at the words homosexual rabbit. 'Not quite. It wasn't so easy. There was a boy at school... We used to masturbate each other under the desk. Even that wasn't till I was seventeen. And though we liked each other, there was no real emotion involved.' He turned and looked into my eyes. I looked into his. I wasn't quite sure what I read there; I only thought, or simply hoped, I knew.

'Sandro wouldn't have known about that, though, I suppose,' I said.

'No,' Michele said. 'But then at university...' This I wanted to hear. 'I fell in love with a boy who was straight. Is straight. He came home with me in the vacations sometimes. My parents didn't spot anything, I think, but Sandro somehow seemed to know. I loved him so much it hurt. He knew that. I'm talking about the boy now, not Sandro. Some of the hurt rubbed off on him. Because he cared about me too. Though not in the way I wanted him to'.

'Once he let me give him a... Oh, what's the word you use? *Una sega...*'

'Una sega?' I didn't know. Michele did a little mime with his fist, just for a split second, while there was no-one in sight in the lane. 'A wank,' I said *Una sega.* My

Italian was coming on in leaps and bounds.

'Out on the lawn, after dark. But that made it somehow worse, more difficult. So near yet so far.'

I felt insanely jealous somehow. Absurdly so. Jealous of someone whose dick Michele had once played with on what I thought of now as our patch of lawn. Jealous of something that happened before I knew who Michele was, before Michele knew me. A ridiculous emotion, but that's the way we're made.

I felt a tremor of sexual excitement pass through me as I asked my next question. A tingle in my shoulders, neck and arms. 'Did he do the same to you?'

Michele shook his head. 'He wouldn't touch mine, though part of him wanted to, I could see. I think he thought it might make him gay. But he stayed and watched as I did my own, standing out there on the lawn.' I saw the picture only too easily in my mind's eye. 'We're still friends, actually. When I came back yesterday from staying with a friend in the mountains – well, that was him.'

Oh, I thought. I felt a cold shock of dismay. I couldn't leave the next question unasked, even though I dreaded what Michele might say in reply. 'And are you still in love with him?' I waited, full of misery.

He looked at me unhappily. 'I don't know,' he said.

Poor Michele, I thought. And then – poor me. What about me? But I felt the need to ask another question. I wondered if Catholic priests in the confessional, or even the Spanish Inquisition, were as tenacious as I was being on this walk through the quiet town. 'Anybody else at university? People you loved? Had sex with – without loving them necessarily?'

'Not really. I had two or three ... wanks ... with other men, just casually. That was about all.'

Again I thought, poor Michele. He'd never blown anyone, or fucked a boy or had another boy enter him. He was nearly a year older than I was, but rather less experienced sexually. Because of that, because of his seniority especially, I would have to tread very carefully with him. Be sensitive to his Italian stallion pride.

We had come out of the alley now and were in the town's – or village's – main square. It was a long narrow one. At the far end of it the lake gleamed silver. We'd somehow missed seeing the sun go down.

We sat outside a bar. Any bar. Michele ordered in Italian this time. *'Due birre, per favore.'* Two beers. Tobias seemed a long time ago.

'The thing is,' Michele said in English, but speaking softly. The bar was full of tourists of all nationalities. Whatever language we might have spoken in, we'd be understood by someone or other if we didn't keep our voices down. 'The thing is, I don't know how things can go on. My being gay, I mean. If Sandro's OK with it, that's one thing. But my parents... The rest of bloody Italy...'

Again I felt a shock of dismay. *How things can go on...* Did Michele mean himself and me? Like we were an item already? I didn't think we'd got that far. Although I wanted... I think I did. I wasn't sure... Or did he just mean, himself as a gay man, and was thinking ahead already to the time after I'd left Italy and he was on his own again, or with someone else?

With a succession of partners. Or trying to get somewhere with this straight guy whose name I didn't know – I only knew that he'd wanked him off once on the lawn...

I felt Michele's hand alight firmly, quite blatantly, on my bare thigh. It was not concealed by the table we were sitting at, but on fairly full view. It seemed he didn't care at this moment if people saw or not.

'Sweetheart,' he said, his voice full of concern. 'What is it?'

'What is what?' I asked him. But by then I knew.

'You're crying,' he said.

And then he was crying too.

It's quite difficult to deal with. Two grown men crying together in public because their emotions have grown suddenly complex and big. We needed to hug each other fiercely and let our tears come out with noisy sobs. We needed to say so much, yet we couldn't. Even if we tried to, we'd hurt ourselves as it all came out.

He squeezed my leg for an instant, then let it go. 'Let's walk down to the water,' he said. We stood up. Michele left coins on the table beside our barely tasted beer.

We walked down the length of the square and all the way to the end of the jetty where the boats tied up between their comings and goings throughout the day. The boats had stopped now. There was no-one on the jetty except ourselves. We sat on the end of it, on the tarmac surface, dangling our legs, our toes just inches above the dark ripples. We looked out at the infinite horizon of the lake, and at the still light sky, in which the evening star was beginning to shine. Michele put his big arm around my shoulder, I put my slightly smaller one round his. We both began to cry again, but properly this time. Each could feel the painful heaves of the other's chest and heart.

There is a song in the middle of Die Schöne Müllerin – one of the ones we hadn't done that night – in which the miller's boy sits for the first time beside the mill stream with the girl he loves. His lover's tears fall into the water like first drops of rain. I thought of that then, because that's how it was for us.

'There's so much I want to say, Michele,' I managed to whimper. (Sandro had been prescient, earlier, with his accidental stumbling on that word.) 'But I don't know how. I don't even know what.'

'I think you do,' Michele said. His words were assured. His tone of voice was not. He sounded like a scared school-kid. Then he said, and his voice was breaking now, 'Are you frightened, Henry?'

'Yes. Very.' It came out as a sob.

'Then I'll try to be brave and say it,' Michele whispered. 'In Italian first, if you'll allow. *Ti amo,* Henry.'

'Ti amo, Michele.' I buried my head in his neck and he nuzzled against mine. Both of us were in full flood with tears.

'I love you, Henry,' he repeated it in English.

I said, 'I love you too.'

SEVEN

We got into the car. Michele didn't start the engine. Instead he unzipped my shorts and pulled out my thickening cock. I did the same to him. Love might be a complicated thing but this was not.

We were both hard within seconds. I undid the fastening above his fly, to open it up further – so I could finger the inside of his groin and wrap my hand around his nice little bollocks. Michele didn't bother with that with me. He started to pull my hard-on back and forth, making my foreskin blink. I said, 'Don't go so fast. I always come too quickly. You'll make me spill. I can't hold it back.' It was true. I was still a little kid in that way. It had been the source of some embarrassment with other people in the past.

Michele said, 'Go ahead and spill it. It doesn't matter. You can go again later. This is just to ... what's the thing you say in English? ... about edge and appetite?'

'Take the edge off my appetite,' I said.

Within half a minute Michele had taken the edge off my appetite very nicely. Though messily. It went all over my shorts.

I went on manfully with Michele for a couple more minutes, but his wasn't ready to come just yet. In the end he stowed himself away, with some difficulty because he was now very big, and we drove back home.

'Will you stay with me tonight?' Michele asked me

as we drew up on the gravel in front of the house. 'I mean in my bed.'

'Yes,' I said.

'I wasn't brave enough to ask you last night,' he said a bit uncomfortably. 'I wanted to, but was afraid we'd get caught. I'm going to have to get braver about a lot of things now.'

'Now?' I queried.

'After what you said to me – what we both said to each other – on the pier back there.' We'd repeated that, both in English and Italian, about two dozen more times on the drive back.

'You're thinking about your parents,' I said. 'I understand that. You're talking about the business of … do you know the expression? … coming out.'

Michele nodded.

'Rome wasn't built in a day,' I said. 'We should be able to manage not to get caught, surely at least for tonight.'

We paid great attention to the details of our deception, even though everyone else was probably asleep. Certainly no-one was still up. We climbed the stairs softly, like cats. We said goodnight quietly, though not in suspicion-garnering lovers' whispers, at the top of the stairs. I opened my door with a soft click, then closed it again with another one. Michele opened his own door, handed me through it, followed swiftly, and shut it again with both of us inside the room. For good measure he then turned the key in the lock.

I'd never thought of kissing as a noisy thing. It's only when you're trying to do everything quietly that you □ealize that, if you're more passionate than careful, it is. We hugged each other and then, still standing, and trying to be quiet about it, kissed. We undressed no further than to undo each other's shorts, allowing gravity to drop them round our ankles, so that our standing dicks could join in the embrace.

And then we went to bed. What a simple statement. But what a hefty deal that is when the bed belongs to the boy with whom you've just fallen in love, and it's the first time for the two of you, together in that place.

Naked we burrowed among the covers, touching, stroking, occasionally, almost accidentally, jabbing each other's groin or tummy with our erect pricks.

'I don't have protectives or anything,' Michele said. He explained a bit shyly, 'I wasn't expecting to have sex with anyone at home this summer. You've caught me on the jump.'

'On the hop,' I corrected him. His English was so very nearly perfect; he made very few mistakes.

'I'm not sure we'd need them,' I suggested. 'If you haven't had penetrative sex with anyone before. Because, for me, I took a test, and got the result two months ago. I was clear. Still am. I haven't had that sort of sex with anyone since.'

But actually, I wasn't feeling like having that sort of sex with Michele just then. Perhaps because of where we were, and being afraid of the noise we might make. Being brave was all very well, and it looked as though one day Michele would have to come out to his parents, whether he went on loving me or not. It wouldn't be easy for him, I knew that. But there would be better ways to do it than by waking them up in the middle of the night while he was having his first fuck.

Michele hadn't spoken following my remark about the Aids test. I guessed he was mulling over the implications of that. But this wasn't the moment to tell him my chequered sexual history. That could wait. I said, 'You know, I don't feel like fucking you or being fucked by you tonight.' I felt a relaxation in his body, and □ealized he was relieved that I'd said that. He probably had the same anxieties about noise and discovery as I had. 'I'd really like to try and do what I've so far failed to do twice. Use my hand to make you come. Last night you had to finish the job yourself.' He snickered at the memory, or at the way I'd expressed myself, or both. I went on, because I was now curious, 'Does it take you a long time when you masturbate by yourself?' I assumed he did do that. Like everybody else.

He laughed. 'It can take a while sometimes. Especially if I've been doing it a lot.' I wondered what *a lot* meant in his case, but decided not to ask. 'But I always get there in the end.'

'And the boy at school? Under the desk?'

'Oh, he got it out of me easily enough,' Michele said breezily. 'And me from him. We were both only seventeen though.'

The way I came, unpredictably, much too soon, it was like I still was seventeen, I thought. I told him that. 'Just go for it,' he said. 'I'll help you if you need it. And if you come again before I get there, so be it. Just let it happen. We don't have to prove anything to each other in that department. We did the big thing already, saying what we said tonight.'

We drew back the covers and Michele lay on the bottom sheet on his back. I half lay, half knelt, on top of him and took his big cock in my hand.

For a time Michele didn't touch my one, sensitive to my concern about coming too soon. But then the sight of it, bouncing away almost in front of his nose, grew too much for him, and he reached up and began to go at me as well. I didn't protest. It's too frustrating, hauling away at another guy's penis while no hand touches your own. Even if you do come too soon.

It was half a minute only, I reckon, before I felt my semen rise inside me. I erupted strongly, throwing soft white lines and spatters all over Michele's broad chest. I didn't care now, that that had happened. Very quietly we both laughed. Then he sat up a little way, just enough to give me a kiss. Meanwhile I carried on tugging at him.

A couple of minutes later Michele said, 'You've nearly done it. I'm almost there.' And he told me, though he had to do this bit in Italian, to pull his foreskin right back with my free hand and, while not stopping my fist action, tickle his exposed cock-head under its chin.

As my free hand was taking my weight at that time it took a bit of effort to accomplish this. I had to fall forward onto my elbow and worm my hand around. But it worked a treat. A moment later the product of Michele's necessarily rather quiet ejaculation had launched itself onto his chest, where its long fine line joined mine.

Never had I had such difficulty in coaxing another boy off by hand. Never had I felt more pleased, more rewarded, with the result.

*

We slept only fitfully, of course. But even that had its good side. To wake up and find someone you love lying beside you is the most wonderful experience in life. To do so six or seven times in one short night is demi-paradise.

At half past five I whispered to Michele, 'I'd better go back to my own room.' He didn't want to let me go but agreed I had to. To leave it longer would be courting too much risk. I got out of bed and kissed him, then put shorts and shirt on and crossed the floor to the door, carrying my shoes.

Silently, turning the handle at the speed of the second hand of a watch, I let myself out onto the landing and, equally slowly, closed the door behind me. Then I froze, rigid with horror. Someone was coming up the stairs.

I had no time to unfreeze or even think of anything to say. The person on the stairs appeared in front of me. And he too froze, rigid with surprise.

It was Sandro, in his socks, and carrying his shoes.

There was a moment's mutual astonishment and then, as Sandro took in my situation and realised whose door I'd just come out of, and as I realised that he must have just come back from a night in bed with Daniela, we had to stop ourselves from falling around in helpless loud guffaws. Instead we grinned hilariously at each other, and simultaneously put a forefinger to our lips. Then Sandro took his finger away from his lips and touched mine with it. I followed suit, touching his soft warm lips with my own finger-end.

It was an eerily sexy moment. If I'd had any lingering doubts as to whether Sandro and I had bonded successfully, they were laid to rest from that moment on. We continued on our arrested, silent, journeys to our respective rooms, walking past each other to do so. As we passed, conspirators in the night, Sandro reached out and rubbed my shoulder lightly and, emboldened, I rubbed his.

*

In the morning we went to Verona, the three of us. Michele drove, and got us there in half an hour. The opera season had started and the town was heaving with tourists. Had it been me trying to park the car I would probably have given up and gone home, but natives Michele and Sandro knew a tucked-away place just over the river, where we left the car and then walked back across the bridge into the old town.

A criss-cross of streets, lined with handsome buildings mostly pink in colour, and dating from the Renaissance and the Middle Ages and back to Roman times. We saw the market of the Piazza del Erbe and the fourteenth-century Gardello tower. We climbed the eight hundred years old Torre dei Lamberti and looked down from its lofty height across the red roofs and heaven-gazing church towers of the town. Around the old town's perimeter the River Adige ran like a necklace, in almost a complete circle, the many bridges over it resembling the links or joints of the chain. The Romans had been wise to found the city here. Securely tucked within its meander of the river, it looked a good place to defend.

And then we came down from our medieval turret and went to see the place to which each and every visitor to Verona finds himself or herself drawn. Number 23, Via Capello. It has a famous balcony, though that was added generations after its story was written, in response to massive demand. La Casa di Giuletta – where Shakespeare's Juliet was wooed by Romeo.

There was more than one layer of disbelief to suspend. The house had indeed belonged to the Capello family – the Capulets of Shakespeare's tale. But the girl and her Montague boyfriend were fiction through and through. Add to that the fact that the famous balcony was placed clearly on the garden side of the house by Shakespeare. *The orchard walls are high and hard to climb.* While the balcony that was erected many years later to represent it looks into a paved courtyard.

Nevertheless, there is a tradition associated with the place – call it superstition if you want to – that I found hard to ignore. Sandro stood there in the courtyard and said it, not looking particularly at either Michele or me or at both of us, but just mentioning it as a passing remark. 'If you have a wish that is connected with love, then go and stand under the balcony and make it. It will come true.'

Michele laughed. He knew this already. I did not. But that story explained the little knot of tourists that came and went beneath the balcony. I'd seen people arrive, stand a moment, giggle at each other in amused embarrassment, then walk away again.

Risking the mocking laughter of Michele and his brother I took a couple of paces away from them and stood under the balcony myself. I closed my eyes a moment. In my head I recited the following words. *I wish that for Michele and me this may be just the beginning. I wish us always to love each other the way we do now.* Well, that was perhaps two wishes, not just one. I didn't know if two were allowed. I certainly wasn't sure I'd be allowed three of them. But I chanced my arm anyway. *I wish that Michele and I will be happy, and together, for ever and ever and ever.*

I felt a touch on my right shoulder, and opened my eyes. Michele stood there, beneath the balcony with me, looking into my eyes. His own eyes were glistening. Perhaps that was the sun. He didn't take his hand off my shoulder. He said, 'May I have the honour of your love for ever, Little One?'

EIGHT

The next day was Friday. Michele was summoned by his father to go with him to the head office of his company, in Trento. They set off after breakfast. On the *autostrada* it meant a journey of half an hour or so, heading north to just beyond the head of the lake.

I had decided, and Sandro agreed, that we should spend the morning revising all that I had taught him, or that he had learnt, to date. This might have meant our sitting cooped up in his bedroom at my insistence, but it did not. I'd learnt from my first morning's mistake, and so I suggested we took his notes, the two dictionaries, pens and paper out with us into the garden. We chose a spot where there was a wooden seat placed strategically, at the edge of the patch of shade that was cast by a spreading cedar of Lebanon. In front of us the bright green lawns cascaded down the hill, and between the sentinel cypress trees the vast mirror of the lake...

'It's doing what, Sandro?' I said.

He chuckled. 'Sparkling, glitterning, glinting and gleaming at us. But not gloating or glowering, I think.'

'Full marks,' I said.

I took his notebook from him, looked at what he'd written there, then questioned him on it, testing gently. He'd been a good student. In just three days his English had come on a lot. By the end of the summer he'd be as good as his brother was, swimming and sporting his way through the currents of the language like a fish.

'Why is business called business?' he asked me out of the blue at one moment. Well, not quite out of the blue. We were discussing the many common words in English that were not pronounced remotely the way they were spelt.

I had to think for a moment. With Sandro's questions I often did. Then I said, 'I think it means busy-ness. Meaning being occupied, working hard. Like a bee. We say that bees are busy in English. Did you know that?'

No, he didn't. But he liked the idea. I told him, 'As busy as a bee.'

'It's nice,' he said. 'It goes with the noise they make. Which makes it … wait … it's the same word in Italian almost, only I can't remember it... Onomatopoeia... Am I right?'

He was. I could only just remember or pronounce the word myself. 'What adjective do you use for bees in Italian?' I asked him.

'We say they are assiduous,' he said. 'Which, if you say it in Italian, especially the adverb form, *assiduoso*, also sounds a bit like bees.'

I agreed. Especially the way he pronounced it, with those lilting Italian cadences of his. I thought just then that it was as well I'd fallen in love with his elder brother, and that his elder brother was gay. Otherwise I'd most certainly have fallen in love with Sandro at this moment. Sandro, sitting smiling in dappled sunlight, beside me on a bench. Sandro who wasn't gay at all. And there'd be nothing but misery ahead.

Then I thought, but there might be misery ahead for

me anyway, with Michele. He was gay (good) and as much in love with me as I was with him (good) but there it ended. He lived in Italy, he wasn't 'out'. He was rich, I was poor by comparison. We'd be parting in seven weeks… Oh my God, just days ago we were talking about eight... What the fuck was going to happen to us? For a moment, despite the lovely sunshine, and the lovely presence of Sandro by my side, my thoughts went black.

I heard Sandro say, very softly, 'You're thinking about 'Chele, aren't you.' He didn't frame it as a question. He just knew. I nodded. I found I couldn't speak.

'It's hard for him,' Sandro went on. 'Easier for me. I've got a girlfriend. That's expected of an Italian boy. It unlocks social doors that will be closed to 'Chele if – excuse me – he continues to fancy you.' It was a brutal way of putting it – Sandro didn't mean it to be, but his English lacked a bit of nuance as yet – yet it was true. Michele's relationship with me, if it continued, would be a hindrance to him.

'Also,' Sandro went on, 'he isn't really interested in the family business. I am.' Michele's father's company was one of the biggest manufacturers of knives, forks and spoons in Italy. 'I love cutlery. It's quite uncomplicated for me. Not for its own … what is it...?'

'Its own sake,' I reminded him.

'But for the money it makes. That's me.' He paused a second and stared out across the bright blue lake. 'But 'Chele's different. Wants to be an opera singer. He won't be happy if he doesn't get the chance.' He stopped again. 'You've heard him sing. I don't know...

What do you think?'

'I think his singing's wonderful,' I said. 'That's not just because I'm in love with him...' Now I stopped. 'I didn't mean to say that to you,' I said shakily. 'It just slipped out.'

Sandro said, 'You were being honest with me. And trusting me with your biggest...' He hesitated, searching for a word that would do. He found one. It wasn't brilliant, but it sort of did. '...Your biggest ... thing... I'm honoured by that.'

I moved back to the firmer ground of Michele's singing voice. The previous evening we'd agreed that we'd go to the opera in Verona one evening. Then I had persuaded a pretend-bashful Michele to fetch from a cupboard in his bedroom the music of some operatic favourites, versions in which the orchestral score had been reduced to piano accompaniments. Playable by me, with a bit of make-do and mend, just about. He had sung ravishingly. His voice, of which he'd shown the intimate gentle side in domestic Schubert two nights earlier, now swelled in response to the challenge laid down by music written for a large opera house. I'd heard the windows shake.

'He must have done years of practice at university, or somewhere,' I said now to Sandro. 'I mean, to have reached a standard like that...'

'It's true,' said Sandro. 'He was in every student opera production there was in Padua all the years he was there. He dragged us all over several times. I'm afraid I didn't appreciate it always. I was too young, I think. But I'm learning a bit more now...' He broke off, realising that he'd started to talk about himself when I needed to hear and talk about Michele. I thought that was wonderful of Sandro. He was very sensitive towards me, and very sweet. 'But student opera is student opera. It's not the same as the professional thing. There's a...' He searched for a word. 'An abysmus?' he guessed.

'A yawning gap,' I offered him. 'Between the two things. A yawning gap.'

He grinned and repeated the expression. 'A yawning gap. I like that.'

He looked at the shadows of the trees in the garden a moment, very carefully. I wasn't quite sure why, until he next spoke. He was using them to tell the time by, instead of looking at his watch. 'It'll be time for a coffee in a minute,' he said. 'But first, do you want to test me on those irregular verbs you gave me on the first morning?' He grinned mischievously.

I covered my face with my hands theatrically. 'I was hoping you'd forgotten that,' I said.

'Test me anyway,' he instructed me. And so I did. Grinning broadly at each other we went through the entire list, beginning with *beget, begat*. It turned out he'd learnt the lot.

*

After lunch we went into Garda village, taking the boat. We dragged it out through the gate in the wall at the bottom of the garden. We'd done the same the first day we went out in it. That gate had been less significant back then. It hadn't witnessed Michele and me passing through it with our cocks poking out of our trousers, and about to make love for the first time.

We got the boat down into the water and then climbed into it. 'I am starting the outboard engine with the pull-cord,' Sandro announced, in the gently mocking tone of someone sending up both his English teacher and himself. 'Now I am setting the throttle. Adjusting it. And I shall allow my friend Henry to take the tiller, and steer us to the harbour in the village.'

My friend Henry was the bit I loved.

I steered all the way to the harbour mole, not too badly. Then Sandro took over, just in case I were accidentally to ram any expensive boats. 'That's ours,' he said, pointing to a small yacht with exceptionally elegant lines.

'I didn't know you had a yacht,' I said. But why not? The family seemed to have everything else.

'We'll go for a sail in it one day soon,' Sandro said. He gave me back the tiller for a moment, while he leapt off the boat with the mooring rope to tie up.

*

There was a long summery cocktail in fashion that year. It was called a Veneziano, and had become popular, Sandro told me, as a result of a successful TV advertising campaign which featured a woman with flame-coloured hair.

It was a flame-coloured cocktail. As we walked along the promenade that afternoon it seemed that just everyone was drinking it. It shone from a hundred glasses, lighting every outdoor table along the half-mile stretch like a blazing lantern: it caught the sun's brilliance along all that parade of glasses and winked it back.

'A cocktail brighter than the orange sun,' Sandro observed. For someone whose avowed interest lay in making money from knives and forks he had a poetic turn of phrase sometimes.

I said, 'Better try one, I suppose.'

It was quite nice. A bit on the sweet side for my taste. But then it would have been difficult for anything to taste quite as astonishing as this drink looked.

With a drink in his hand, sitting under an awning and looking out over the sparkling afternoon lake, Sandro changed his role. From being my little pupil, he metamorphosed into my big brother. In the nicest way, of course. In the way that Michele was his. 'You will have to be careful,' he said. 'The two of you. Sleeping together in Michele's room night after night.'

'It's only been two nights,' I objected stupidly. (We'd slept in Michele's bed again last night. Again we'd been quiet about it. I'd left before dawn, like Romeo. I hadn't met Sandro on the stairs this time. But he knew anyway.)

'Yes, but you won't stop at that. That's not possible, is it.'

I agreed that it was not.

'Then one day you'll get caught.'

'Not necessarily,' I said. 'You can play the lottery for years and never win a euro.'

'That's not the same,' said Sandro. 'The chances are small when it's about good things happening. When it's bad things, they're big. You're older than me. You must know that.'

It was true. I was older than him. I did know that.

'You need to think about what will happen when our parents catch you. And if they don't... Well, you told me this morning you were in love with 'Chele. 'Chele may not have told me he's in love with you, but it's all over his face.' He stopped and a smirk appeared about his lips. 'And once, on the boat back from Gardone, all over his shorts.' He went on, more seriously, 'Not to mention what happened in Verona yesterday. Underneath the balcony. At some point you'll both have to tell them what's going on. Because, at the end of the summer... What's going to happen then?'

'I don't know,' I blurted wretchedly. Tears sprang to my eyes. 'I don't fucking know, Sandro. Neither does Michele. You got any ideas?'

'Well, 'Chele could tell them he's gay and going to marry you in England, then they could disinherit him and I'd get the company one day outright. That would be nice.' I looked at him appalled. A grin swarmed over his face. 'I'm joking, Henry. You know me better than that.'

'It's just that I can't imagine what's going to happen,' I said. 'I've been trying not to think about it. So has he. It's like we're living in the Garden of Eden at the moment – only knowing that one day we're going to get slung out.'

'Well, one thing that's going to happen that I can think of,' Sandro said, 'is that our parents are going to think it strange that 'Chele keeps coming out with us during my lesson time. I know it's not long after the end of university for him, but they'll soon expect him to go and get some sort of a job, or else muck in a bit more at the company. That's why Babbo took him off to Trento this morning I think. It's not like he was always spending time with me on his other vacations. They'll soon see it's you he wants to be with – even if they don't catch you at it in bed.' He paused. 'He takes a very long time to ejaculate, don't you think?'

I nearly jumped out of my chair. 'How the hell do you know that?'

He laughed. 'Don't worry. It's not as bad as you think. I watched him playing with himself on the lawn once – when I was much younger. He thought no-one was about but I was behind the trees.'

'You were a peeping Tom, then,' I said, and laughed. 'If you know what that means.'

'I can guess,' he said, and laughed back. 'Anyway, it took him an age to get there that time.'

'It still does,' I said. 'Unlike me,' I added without thinking. 'I'm ridiculously quick.'

'So am I,' Sandro admitted. 'I keep hoping it's something I'll grow out of. But what you say about you doesn't give me too much hope.'

We looked at each other and smiled, but a bit awkwardly this time. Here was another bond between us. It was one of those moments that catch people unexpectedly. The first hint of anything between Sandro and me that had to do with sex. I didn't count the fingers-on-each-other's-lips thing, or the shoulder-rubs. Or should I count them? I looked doubtfully at Sandro. He looked equally uncertainly at me. It was like something odd had happened between us. Neither of us was sure what it was exactly. But we were both uncomfortable with it.

We were saved from ourselves or from each other a moment later by the arrival at our table of an exceptionally beautiful girl with auburn hair, a bright blue bandanna, and sunglasses. She was Daniela, and we were introduced.

'You are the friend of Michele,' she said, with a laugh in her voice, as we shook hands. From the corner of my eye I saw Sandro giving urgent shakes of his head. 'Sorry, I mean...' she said, aware that she'd let slip a bit of private pillow-talk. '...I meant to say the teacher of English Sandro's.'

'It's OK,' I said. 'I *am* 'Chele's friend.' The diminutive his family used had slipped out by accident. I'd never used it before. 'I'm also Sandro's friend, I hope.'

Daniela sat with us sipping a coffee while we finished our Venezianos. We talked, in a mixture of English and Italian. The week's English studies were as good as ended, so I didn't chide my pupil when he slid into Italian for his girlfriend's sake. Her English was like my Italian. Only so-so. In that respect she and I were a pretty good match.

I hadn't explored the village of Garda yet, off the waterfront. 'It's very small,' Sandro said, and Daniela laughed. 'But we shall show you it.' They walked me through a pretty archway in an ancient wall, with a clock in the tower above it. We walked down picturesque alleys that had tourists in them but not too many. We stopped and looked at shops.

An ice-cream shop caught my eye. Its window held ice creams of every imaginable flavour and colour. I said, 'I've been in Italy nearly a week and I haven't had an ice-cream yet.'

'It is in-credible!' Daniela trilled. And Sandro pulled his wallet from his pocket and said, 'Then we shall make up for that at once.'

NINE

We slept separately that night. Sandro's words had put the wind up me. And when I relayed them to Michele later that evening outside the Loggia della Losa they put the wind up him too. Still, we made love pretty nicely out in the night-scented garden on our way back to the house.

Which words of Sandro's had worried me most? Pretty well all of them. I passed most of what we'd talked about on to Michele. The only major thing I didn't share with him was that Sandro and I had had an intimate if brief discussion about the inconvenient ejaculatory habits of our cocks.

It was strange to sleep in my own bed again, and to wake up missing Michele's head on the pillow beside me and wondering for a second where he was. But it got better from then on. He was on the other side of the wall, I quickly realised: no further away than that. In a few minutes we would both be getting dressed, emerging from our adjacent doors, even if probably not at the same moment, and meeting over breakfast.

It was Saturday. Sandro and I would be taking a break from each other's company. He to spend the day with Daniela, me to spend it with Michele. 'What will your parents think?' I'd asked him as we sat outside the Loggia last night.

High on the prospect of outdoor sex in half an hour, he'd answered, 'Let them think what they like.'

At breakfast Signora Luccini asked in the casual way that mothers do, which is actually not casual at all, what everyone's plans were for the day. Michele spoke for everyone. 'Sandro's going out with Daniela, I think. And I'll take care of Henry. Probably go for a walk this morning. Let the rest of the day take care of itself.'

His mother looked at me very searchingly. 'Are you happy with that, Henry? Do say if you'd rather be doing something else.'

I met her gaze with a steady, though I hoped friendly, look. 'There's nothing I'd like to do more, actually. I'm very happy with that.'

It wasn't a big 'coming-out' moment. But for both of us it was a first step. I wasn't quite sure if I saw this, but I think that Sandro, sitting next to his mother, gave his brother a wink.

I'd bought myself a backpack from a knick-knack shop in Piazza Catullo. It was very small and neat. If you examined it closely you could see what it really was: a school satchel for a little girl. But nobody was going to examine it closely. From any distance it looked cool and practical. Ideal for taking with you on a walk when you were carrying little more than a bottle of water and some sun-cream.

Michele and I were both wearing khaki shorts again (clean ones today). Deck shoes without socks and – quite by coincidence – very similar pastel blue short-sleeved tops. Nothing else. Not even beneath the shorts.

Apart from that we didn't look alike, of course. Michele with his fair hair, dark designer-stubble beard and eyebrows, and his blue eyes. Me with my darker hair... English boy, Italian boy: it's supposed to be the other way round. But we happened to be real people, not stereotypes.

The shorts were deliberate, the blue tops were not. Yet people would look twice as they passed us, noticing the way we'd dressed. Most would never give a thought to whether we might be a couple. Though just a few, people who were clued up about such matters, gay people for instance, or people who knew about gay people, would. I wondered about Michele's mother. There had been that look she gave us both after Michele sang, and I played, Schubert. And after this breakfast time... I was pretty certain that by now she knew about us.

We unlocked the gate in the garden wall, passed through it, and then for the first time, turned right onto the lakeside path rather than left. Michele said, 'It's time you told me about the others.'

'Other whats?' I asked.

'Other boys you've had.'

'Oh those,' I said. They hardly seemed to matter now. 'I've told you about Tobias,' I said.

'I meant before that.'

'I went to boarding school,' I said. 'There was plenty of opportunity for sex there, for those that wanted it...'

'And did you?'

'Yes, I did,' I said. 'Though there was less opportunity for love.'

'You might not have been old enough for that,' Michele said gently, wisely. 'Anyway, tell me about the sex.'

'OK,' I said. It seemed a pleasantly uncomplicated, water-under-the-bridge thing to be talking about while walking along a sun-swept beach. I told him about my first ever taste of sex with someone else. 'It was a boy called Peter Mills. I suppose I'd always liked the look of him, though without knowing that was the case or what it meant. He was a year above me so we didn't have much to do with each other. Till one week we were both in the sick bay together. Sick bay … it's like a school mini-hospital if you like. It was some tummy bug or other. Tummy bug... Bacteria or virus in the stomach, making you sick.

'I was fifteen, he one year older. I was a bit in awe of him. He made a great show of himself when he got in and out of his bed, showing off his cock, sort of pretend-accidentally but in fact quite deliberately. I tried not to let it show that I was interested but I wasn't that good an actor, so of course he could see that I was.'

'Some things are beyond the skills of even the best actors,' said Michele, deadpan, not breaking his stride.

'Anyway, one night I was nearly asleep when I heard him get out of his bed and come over to mine. Somehow I knew what was going to happen, and I also knew I was going to let it happen, even if I didn't know exactly what *it* was going to be.

'He knelt down beside my bed, and then he said, "Henry," very softly. I heard myself say his name. "Peter." That seemed to have an effect on us both. He reached with his hand under the bedclothes and put his hand on my chest. I didn't move, so he drew his hand down me, opening my pyjama buttons one by one as he went. Then he did the same with the cord that fastened the trousers, and by the time he'd done that he'd already brushed against my cock which was standing right there. I let him wank me and I very quickly came – as always – in a flood that soaked the top sheet. I'd never come so much before. I remember being more worried about the top sheet than anything else. I didn't do anything to him. He didn't seem to expect me to.

'Next morning I didn't know how to look at him, but he remained friendly and was confident and cheerful with me. So he won me over. In the afternoon he invited me into his bed. And I joined him. That time we both did it to each other. And we went on doing that for the rest of the two or three days we were in sick bay together. We were actually disappointed when we were pronounced well enough to go back into school again. It was a real wrench for both of us. We only managed to do it a few more times after that, standing up behind bushes in the dark. Anyway, at the end of that term he left.'

'And that was that,' said Michele.

'Yes,' I said.

'You didn't get your first fuck at school then,' Michele enquired politely.

'No, that came later,' I said. 'At university.' I paused. 'I haven't had my first fuck with you yet.'

Michele said, 'I haven't yet had my first fuck.'

I thought about the sun-cream in my school-girl backpack, and wondered if today would change all that.

We were walking towards the Punta del Vigilio. From the boat going to Gardone, or from the promenade in Garda, it looked like a straight-line walk. But now we were actually doing it I found that we were walking around the edges of a series of little coves and headlands, each one its own little surprise. In places there were reeds taller than we were, through which the path, now sandy, made zigzags. In other places we were scrambling over low rocks. Elsewhere thick tangles of shrub and cypress came right down to the edge of the lake... I thought about the opportunities these different shelters might afford us on the walk back.

Not knowing what is around the next corner is one of the things that keeps us interested in life. And it kept me interested in this particular walk – my joy in being with Michele being too obvious to need repeating at this point. He knew, of course, what lay around each and every corner, but teasingly refused to divulge this knowledge to me. He would know when we reached the Punta, but until we rounded the last of many headlands I did not.

And I wasn't sure what to expect. I didn't feel we were dressed for the kind of high-class joint where Prince Charles stayed, and wondered what would happen when we arrived at... well, wherever we were going to arrive.

We turned a sharp corner where a stone wall materialised and formed a curve. The northern arm of the lake opened out in front of us suddenly, and we saw the north-west shore. We went on, ploughed through unpromising scrub a hundred yards or so, and were then stopped by a wall.

Steps led up. We climbed them. And on the other side the most civilised scene lay right in front of us.. An old house, like a farm or mill. A tiny harbour right beside it no bigger than a town garden, and, along its jetty a row of tables with white cloths on, at which a few, but not too many, people sat in the sunshine drinking coffee or beer. Within seconds we had added to their number by two.

'Thank you,' I said to Michele. 'I had no idea...'

'I did,' said Michele. 'I knew this was here. Quite obviously. But as for what happens from now on today...' He placed his hand firmly on my bare knee, then took it away again. 'Then I have no idea.'

For now the moment was enough. Sunshine. A sun-bright glass of beer. Sitting at a table with a lake – with ducklings on it – flowing on either side of you. Michele within touching distance... We did touch. An instant at a time only, when other people were looking away. We couldn't keep our hands off each other by this stage... And Michele's smile.

I said, 'Michele, is it all right if I call you 'Chele? Kayley, like your brother does.'

'You could call me anything you want,' he said. 'I'd answer to it if it came from you.'

''Chele,' I said simply. Just testing it, like you do with a microphone.

'Is there anything short you'd like me to call you?'

he asked.

I hadn't thought about it. Henry's pretty short already. Not even my mother had ever thought to shorten it. Nor had my friends – or even enemies – at school.

I said, on the spur of the moment, 'Call me Hen.'

'Hen? Like the bird?'

'Exactly,' I said. 'Like the bird.'

'Like the bird? I love him.' He beamed, surprised at his own cleverness. I think it was the first time he'd attempted a play on English words. 'And hen's the right bird for me anyway,' he added.

'Why's that, then?' I said.

Michele's beaming smile grew broader. 'Because you won't fly too far away.'

A little boat chugged into view from behind the wall of the house. It was the kind of small motor launch that I'd been out in with Sandro twice. We watched idly as it approached the entrance of the minuscule harbour on whose wall we sat. It nosed its way in.

There were two men on board. Had they been shorts-wearing, bronze-thighed guys of twenty, naked to the waist I could describe them minutely at this point. Because they didn't come into that category I can't. I hardly noticed them, to tell the truth. Fine police witness I'd make.

They approached the wall of the jetty directly beneath us. There were mooring rings set in the wall.

We could see them where the wall curved towards the harbour entrance. The ones below us were out of sight, of course, but the men in the boat were clearly aiming for one of them, as one stood up in the bow, his fist clenched on a length of rope.

Did he make a sudden move that affected the boat's balance? Did they hit some obstruction in the water beneath them? In the middle of this idyllic scene, in the middle of our peaceful beer and affectionate banter the most amazing thing occurred in front of us, below us. It was almost impossible to believe it was happening, as we watched.

The little boat tipped sideways violently. For a split second we saw it surreally sticking up sideways, while the two men crashed into the water with a pair of shouts. A split-second later the boat was upside down, keel uppermost, and the two men had disappeared from sight.

Michele leaped to his feet. He swore in Italian. I didn't know the word. He didn't wait to strip his top off, or remove his watch. He took the single step necessary to get him to the edge, kicked his shoes off and then he jumped. Down into the water, feet first.

I leapt out of my chair – out of astonishment and fright. Took my one step to the edge. Like Michele I didn't pause to take my top off. I even forgot to kick off my deck shoes. Apart from that detail I followed 'Chele's example to the letter. I jumped, while the water was still resounding with his splash.

I was amazed at the amount of thinking I had time for in the space between my take off into the air and my watery touchdown. First, I was astonished at myself for doing this. I'd never thought I was the kind of guy to go rescuing people from water. Second, I realised I was doing this only because of 'Chele. Because I wanted to be worthy of him, and because I was ready to follow him wherever he went. Over broken glass if necessary. Jaws of hell and back. The third thought that had time to come to me was the very good reason why I wasn't the kind of guy who goes jumping into deep water to pull unfortunate people out: it was because I couldn't swim.

TEN

I think I was too frightened to listen out for my own splash. I certainly don't remember hearing it. The things I did know were: I was standing fully clothed in very cold water up to my chest; my feet, from which the shoes had somehow been torn off were sliding around, trying to keep me upright, in thick mud; I wasn't alone, though: there were four of us, standing around, and holding onto, an upturned boat. I wouldn't be having to swim for it, or rescue anyone, thank God.

Somehow we got the boat the right way up, the four of us. Somehow there wasn't too much water in it. Somehow we waded with it the last two metres towards the wall and tied it up. Somehow I found my shoes by poking about with my feet. I reached down and retrieved them. I kept my mouth closed while I did this, but some water still got up my nose.

There were steps cut in the wall nearby. Other people were on them, reaching down, offering us their hands, hauling us up.

Moments later we were sitting at our table again. It seemed incongruous to see our beer glasses still sitting there unperturbed, as if nothing had happened. Though now there were four of us. The other men were in their forties or fifties, I guessed. That detail seemed irrelevant. There is a great equality between people who are all soaking wet and have shared a bit of a fright.

Waiters were running towards us with towels. Wet wallets and phones were being laid on the table and inspected for damage. Everybody was talking at once, and waving their arms about. All in Italian, of course. I let it all wash over me. I wondered whether to put my wet shoes back on or not.

We all pulled our tops off, and towelled our hair and upper halves. Then there was a bit of a pause as we each wondered what to do about the bottom half. Michele took the lead. He had nothing to lose except his shorts. I followed his example. (How often I seem to be writing this sentence now!) And then, a bit more sheepishly the other men did the same. After a minute or two of that familiar but never easy exercise of drying ourselves while preserving our modesty with one and the same towel, we were all sitting back down again, towels wrapped around our nakedness, while our clothes lay on the edge of the jetty, drying as best they could in the sun. The two men ordered coffee and Grappa. 'Chele and I reconnected with our beer.

Conversation resumed. I was still a bit on the outside of it. The streams of Italian flowed very fast, so that I could only get snatches of what was said. The difficulty was increased because nobody waited for anyone else to finish before jumping in. I did gather at least that the two men from the boat were extremely grateful to us, and would like to reward us in some way.

After a moment Michele turned to me and said in English, 'Do you realise who these people are?' We'd exchanged names a minute earlier, but the new ones hadn't rung any bells with me. 'Signor Grippi is the director of Opera Vicenza.' He didn't say what the other one did. But I'd concluded from the way they looked at each other, and their body language, that the two of them were a bit more than just good friends. Michele went on, 'They're doing Rigoletto in the

Arena in Verona in two weeks' time.'

The others must have caught the excitement in Michele's voice. They asked if we liked the opera. I said yes, of course, even though it wasn't my biggest musical passion. But it was something Michele loved, so I was beginning to like it more now.

'Then may we offer you tickets for Rigoletto the week after next?' Signor Grippi said. It was in Italian, but I understood perfectly.

We said yes and thank you, naturally. Then I heard myself saying, excitedly, *'Michele canta bene. Molto bene. Molto molto bene.'* My Italian wasn't up to elaborating on this, as you'll already have spotted, so I relapsed into English and hoped for the best. 'He's absolutely brilliant. I've played his accompaniments. I've heard him in Puccini, Verdi and Mozart. He makes the windows rattle, and it's not a small house. If you really want to thank us, please audition him. I don't ask anything for myself. Just that for him.'

The two men exchanged a glance I couldn't interpret. Michele groaned. 'Hen, no. Don't!' Then he covered his blushing face with his hands and in the process nearly lost his towel.

Signor Grippi leaned towards me across the table. He said in impeccable English, 'Michele is a very lucky man to have a friend who cares for him as selflessly as you obviously do. A lucky man indeed. I hope he appreciates you.' He smiled. He turned to Michele. 'Have you ever sung in public? In a bigger space than your *not small* house?'

Michele had recovered himself just sufficiently to answer. He reeled off a list of roles he'd sung as a student in Padua, and named the buildings in which he'd appeared on stage.

'The problem is,' Signor Grippi said, 'and I hope it won't surprise you to be told, that there are no vacancies in the company at present, and we're not expecting any in the short term.'

I interrupted. Rude of me, I know, but sometimes... I said, 'But please, just audition him anyway. Then you'd remember him in the future when a vacancy arose.'

Grippi looked at me, an amused look on his face. 'You have a touching faith in your friend's powers.' I took that as the mild rebuke it probably was. But then he turned back to Michele. 'Sing something to me now.'

'What?' 'Chele sounded appalled.

'Anything you like,' Grippi said.

And so 'Chele, clad in nothing but a damp towel, sitting on a harbour wall that had just turned gypsy encampment thanks to our cast-off, drying clothes, pulled himself together with a deep breath and – probably because Rigoletto was the opera that had just been mentioned – launched into La donna è mobile with the full force of his open lungs. Not everyone may know the name of the aria, but everyone on the planet knows how it goes.

Every head at every nearby table turned to look, like heads at a tennis game. Those too far away to see Michele clearly stood up to get a view.

I thought Grippi would stop Michele after a few

bars. Probably Michele thought that too. Because his eyes widened a bit as he went on singing. I began to worry, not knowing if he'd know all the words right through to the end.

But he did know them. He sang the aria right through, reached the end and stopped. Grippi exchanged another unreadable look with his friend. He turned to Michele. 'Well, you certainly can sing.' He turned to me and said, with a little laugh in his voice, *'Si, signor. Michele canta molto molto bene.'* Then he returned his attention to Michele. 'Yes. I will give you an audition. Your friend's persistence has paid off. And, in tough circumstances, you acquitted yourself very well just now. An audition is not a job, though, as of course you know. But it's a beginning. Bring me two or three contrasting things.' He chuckled. 'And yes, La donna è mobile can be one of them. One day towards the end of next week.' He waved his hands around in the vicinity of his naked chest. 'I don't have my diary on me. You'll have to phone my secretary to fix a date and time.'

We stayed and had a second drink with Signor Grippi and his friend. Then we struggled back into our half dry shorts again under our towels. I was conscious of something I hadn't given a thought to when we were removing them. That there were no underpants beneath them. And that went for both of us. But now I suddenly realised we were making a rather public statement that we weren't wearing any. And I saw, from a little surprised start that both of them made, that our new friends had clocked that too.

We said goodbye, returned our towels, and Michele entered Signor Grippi's office number in his – surprisingly still working, so probably expensive –

phone.

Then we began to retrace our morning's route. Down the steps, across the little expanse of scrubby beach, and round the corner by the wall, until we were in sight again of Garda and the south-eastern shore.

The same route, the same steps, but somehow we were different people. I understood now why, in religions throughout the world, baptism by immersion in water is a symbol of being re-born.

It was as though our love had undergone a test, and we'd come through it. I'd jumped into water I wouldn't have been able to swim in if it had come to it. Michele had launched himself even before that out of a selfless desire to help people he didn't know. He'd then had the balls to sing the most famous aria from Rigoletto at the top of his voice, without rehearsal, warm-up or piano accompaniment, wearing nothing but a sodden towel, with water trickling from his hair.

As I was thinking that I heard Michele say, 'You know, I wouldn't have – couldn't have – done any of that except for you.'

'What? Sung the song?'

'Any of it. I wouldn't have had the courage to jump into the water, I don't think. But you were there. And so I did.'

I said, 'I only jumped into the water because of you. I wanted to impress you. I wanted to be worthy of you.'

He said, with wonder in his voice, 'But it was just the same for me.' He paused. 'Lucky the water wasn't deep, though. I don't swim very well.'

I said, 'I can't really swim at all.'

'Christ, you were brave, then.'

'Like I said,' I said, 'I only did it because of you. If you hadn't done it first, set the example, I wouldn't have had the balls.'

'Lucky for me that you do have the balls,' Michele said. He made a playful grab for them through my shorts. He then put his hand into my pocket and burrowed down to feel them, and my penis, better, and for quite some time – there was no-one walking towards us for just that bit, we walked along like that.

'And I've got an audition,' he said a minute later. 'I have you to thank for that. Entirely you.' A pause. Then, 'Will you help me rehearse my pieces?'

'Of course,' I said. 'Apart from the time I have to spend with Sandro you can count on me for every minute of every day.'

With a straight face he said, 'Apart from all those moments when you and I have better things to do.'

'We passed a place on the way here,' I said, 'where I thought we might find better things to do on the way back. We're just coming up to it.'

It was a little pathway that led up over stones to a grassy spot in the shade of trees. We went up there. We were quite alone. If anybody started to come up the path towards us I knew we'd hear them scrambling over the stones.

We stood in the shade of one of the trees. Michele wormed his hand between my top and my shorts and hooked his fingers down behind the waistband. 'Breathe in.'

I did, and his hand went all the way down. My cock was small and flaccid, but he played with it and fondled it as if it was a little furry animal, and in no time at all it wasn't small and flaccid any more.

We were almost naked anyway. Just shorts and a flimsy blue top to remove each. But remove them we did, and a minute later were looking approvingly at each other's bare forms. Michele's erection, bigger than mine at the best and worst of times, was now the biggest I'd ever seen it. The sunshine played its part in that, I have no doubt. But he'd grown enormously in confidence in the last two hours. Leaping to the rescue as he'd done, then singing superbly, dressed in a towel... It was as if he'd grown physically in stature. Well, obviously he hadn't. He'd been six foot one when he woke up this morning and he was still six foot one. Though he now looked about ten feet tall.

You can't add a cubit to your height, of course, but the size of one's dick is a more elastic thing. Michele was – I had no doubt about it – sporting the longest and thickest hard-on he'd ever had in his life.

And mine was not too bad.

'Lie down,' Michele told me, gently, but meaning it. I did as I was told. 'We've been in water since we last put sun-cream on,' he said. 'Should we give that another go?'

We did, and it was more than lovely. We rubbed the cream all over each other, paying particular attention to... Well, you know which bits. We were lying and rolling about on grass, so of course bits of grass got all mixed up in it, and soon there was quite a bit of it stuck to ourselves. We didn't care.

I knew what was going to happen. I also knew that, this first time anyway, Michele would be in charge. I rolled onto my back and spread my legs a little by way of invitation, then Michele rolled round and lay front-down on top of me. I saw him reach sideways for the sun-cream, then his hand, with the sun-cream bottle, disappeared from view. I heard the squeezy noise of the plastic bottle, though I didn't need the evidence of my ears to know what he had done. It felt almost as if he'd already come inside me. Except that it felt bloody cold.

Considering he'd never had this done to him, he seemed pretty assured about knowing what to do. Perhaps it's one of those things you don't need teaching – although I'd had to be shown the way the first time round. Of course, you can learn a lot from videos.

I'd only had two cocks inside me before, although both of them a good few times. Neither of them had been anything like as big as this. And yet 'Chele eased his plunger into me without difficulty or discomfort. A hell of a lot of sun-cream must have been involved.

When he'd got all the way in he stopped a moment. 'I'm happy we're doing it this way round,' he said. 'This way I can look into your eyes.'

His face looked more beautiful at that moment than I'd ever seen it. I said, 'And I can look into yours.'

He began to make inch-long pulls and thrusts inside me. After a minute he grew bolder, lengthening his stroke, and setting up a steady rhythmic plunge. I settled back, prepared for the probability that this would take some time.

He squeezed a hand between us and clasped my hidden but very much still-there dick. 'Do you want me to wank you?' he asked me quietly.

I said, 'No. Hold off for a bit. I've got a better idea. If I can last out.' Though it was a very big if.

Then, to my surprise, he came suddenly: turning himself into one big six-foot-one piston, he thrust urgently a dozen times, and his whole body spasmed. I felt his cock swell and pulse inside me as he filled me with his sperm.

He didn't pull out immediately. I didn't want him to. We lay together, two grown-up gilded cherubs, his long hard cock inside me; we were two heavenly conjoined twins.

ELEVEN

We stayed where we were for half an hour, and then Michele eased his way gently out of me. No-one had come by to disturb us: a lucky state of affairs for a summer Saturday afternoon. I said, 'Would you let me do the same to you?' I wasn't sure he'd say yes to that, as he was very much top dog now, since this morning's adventures, and besides, he'd shot his own load only half an hour ago. So I was almost surprised to hear him say,

'Yes. Of course I would.' But then he added, 'You mean now?'

I glanced down at myself. Things didn't look too promising. My dick had regressed to square one. But faint heart never got anyone anywhere. I said, 'Yes, I do mean now. Well, in a minute or two.'

He said, 'Let me help you with that.' And though I was terrified of losing the day before I'd started, he teased me back to hardness with his hand.

I've written so many times that I did exactly as Michele had done, and so I don't need to spell out again exactly what happened after that. Enough to say that I followed his example in every detail, including the hefty initial squirt of sun-cream. Once inside him, and gazing down into his china-blue eyes, I knew that I'd come quickly. And after a minute or so I did. I was just grateful, though, that I'd lasted as long as I had.

'I hope I didn't hurt you,' I said, as I pulled out.

'No,' he said. 'You didn't. Although I don't think I'd

have minded if you had.' He didn't mention the fact that I wasn't all that enormous; I was grateful to him for that. 'The sun-cream works brilliantly.'

I had just pulled out of him, remember, but I was still lying on top of him, between his spread legs, my bottom on full view. We didn't hear anyone coming. I must have been coming myself at the moment when he scrambled over the stones. And neither of us saw him heave into view. It was his voice that alerted us to his presence, as he said in English, 'Well well, you naughty boys...'

I rolled back off Michele as quickly as if I'd had an electric shock. It wasn't the most sensible move I could have made, as I'd now unwittingly exposed both my own hard cock and 'Chele's to the sunlight and our visitor's gaze.

'Sandro!' Michele called out. And then the Italian equivalent of, 'What the fuck are you doing here?'

In horror I looked around me for Daniela. I realised that Michele was doing the same. Be thankful for small mercies, I told myself. Daniela wasn't there.

'Daniela had to go home for something,' Sandro said calmly. 'I'm just out for a stroll. And you two?' A cheeky grin appeared on his face. 'How have you been spending the day?'

Sandro was dressed in shorts and T-shirt. A minute later so were we. We all walked back together along the shore of the lake. There was much to tell Sandro, and he was suitably astounded. However extraordinary our tale was, and however much he was impressed, I thought it unlikely that it would banish from his mind for ever the memory that he'd caught us putting the finishing touches to our first-ever-time-together mutual fuck.

As we walked together, the three of us, I found myself discovering a kind of quiet thrill. At the idea that Sandro had seen me naked and with a good hard-on. And then the naughty thought ran through my mind that I'd rather like to see him in that state too.

*

'An audition with Opera Vicenza?' Signora Luccini was not only astonished and impressed, but mightily pleased with her elder son. And then Sandro told her the story of the plunge into the water because Michele was too modest to do it, and I felt too shy. She didn't look at Sandro's face as she listened to his words but looked searchingly into the faces of her other son and me, flicking second by second from one to the other of us. She seemed to be living the scene, and seeing it all happen in front of her. But I felt she was seeing more than that. I felt that, with a mother's insight and as a woman who knew, like Schubert's mill stream in the song, *what love does*, she realised clearly that what Michele had done he had done for me, and that what I had done, I had done for him.

Despite the loveliness of the afternoon and the call of the outdoors, we spent the rest of the afternoon in the salon where the piano was, frantically choosing, then starting to work on, Michele's audition songs. It wasn't a hardship to forego the sunshine. By this stage I'd have rehearsed in a dungeon if 'Chele had asked me to. And this wasn't a dungeon but a high ceilinged, elegantly furnished space. And all the tall windows and French doors were open anyway. At one moment while we were working a swift flew in, its dark scimitar wings a blur. It did a couple of circuits of the room, made its little trademark screeching sound and flew back out again.

There was a sort of suppressed hysteria at dinner. Even 'Babbo' was caught up in the spirit of the new situation: Michele on the road – maybe, maybe – to becoming an opera star.

Later, Michele drove us – the three of us, for little brother came too – down to the Garda waterfront in the Aventador. Daniela joined us there. Nothing was said to Daniela about what Sandro had witnessed – and what he'd not quite witnessed – earlier. Though I knew full well it would be as soon as Michele and I weren't there.

And when bedtime came, Michele invited me into his room again to spend the night with him. It seemed our confidence had returned.

*

In the morning, which was Sunday, the whole family went to church. I wasn't a believer, neither were the two boys: we'd discussed that matter earlier in the week. But Michele and Sandro went dutifully most Sundays during the holidays, out of loyalty to their parents. And I'd been reliably informed that Signor Luccini, who wasn't a believer either, went out of loyalty to his. While I tagged along on this occasion because, where Michele went, I had to be too. It occurred to me that church-going might always have been like this. And everywhere.

I'd never been to a Roman Catholic Mass before. It was a bit of an eye-opener. There were bells, and smells of incense, and green, gold-embroidered robes.

A very stately ceremony with a rhythm of its own. And, because formal Italian's so much like Latin, I had the feeling of taking part in, or at least observing, something that had been going on unchanged, day after day, for two thousand years.

That said, it was a rather long service and I was relieved, when it was over, to get out in the sunshine again. The little church was sited by a small bridge which crossed a stream. Looking down over the parapet as we crossed it I saw fish in it, hovering in the current, waving their translucent tails.

We walked a couple of hundred yards from there, through the village alleyways, to the waterfront, to the Piazza Catullo, where we had lunch at the Piccolo Hotel. The hotel was small, as its name signified. A handsome little building with red ochre paintwork. We didn't go indoors. Small it might be inside but its outdoor tables ran all the way from one end of the Piazza to the other: from the landward end right down to the lake. It was said to offer the best food along the Garda lake-front. After lunch − home-made tortelloni with truffles, a T-bone steak, then an inevitable tiramisù − I had no reason to doubt the claim.

It was a long and leisurely lunch. We were sitting right by the lake's edge. It was the best spot to be in, but it meant the waiters and waitresses had to walk miles every time they brought us drinks or food. But, I told myself, that went with the job. And it explained the happy fact that young waiters were always slim.

Signor Luccini asked us, at the end of the meal, what we were all doing with the rest of the afternoon. He wasn't being nosy; he simply wanted to know who he would be driving the short distance back to the house, and who wanted to stay in Garda. Sandro said he was going up to Daniela's place later. He'd like a lift back home first. That would take him three quarters of the way.

After a quick interrogative glance at me, Michele spoke for both of us. We'd stay down in the village, and walk back along the shore as and when.

I saw something cross the face of Luccini senior that might have been the shadow of a frown. 'Isn't it time you got yourself a girlfriend again, 'Chele? Maybe you should give our friend Henry a chance to find one too while he's in Italy. Instead of cramping his style.'

His wife interrupted him then, thank Heaven. Had I spoken, or had 'Chele, we'd have said stupid things. Instead, she said smoothly, 'I think it's rather wonderful that Henry and 'Chele get on so well. You've heard them play and sing together. The chemisty between them is very special.' She peered at her husband. 'You must have noticed that. Besides, it's doing wonders for 'Chele's English –and Henry's Italian – without any money changing hands. Don't ask 'Chele to go looking for something he may not want. I think it's rather lovely that 'Chele – and Henry – have both found a friend.'

She knew when to stop, did Signora Luccini, and she stopped then. Her husband found he had nothing more to say.

*

We sat together by the water's edge, Michele and I. At one of the quieter points between the rose and jasmine promenade and our own gate in the wall. We had taken our shoes off and were letting the wavelets lap over our bare feet and cool them. We weren't in shorts but in light blond chinos. We'd dressed for Mass after all, and Sunday family lunch. We were good boys. We even had underwear on.

'What did you make of that speech of your mother's?' I asked 'Chele.

'I think it means she knows.'

'Knows how much, though?' I asked, a bit rhetorically.

He answered equally rhetorically, 'Who ever knows how much their mother knows?' Then he suddenly found fault with something in himself. 'Oh shit. You'll think me really uncaring for not asking you this before. I should have done. Obviously. Are you out to your parents? How are they about you?'

I laughed, I'm afraid. He did like to beat himself up over nothing. Too well bred by half. Endlessly imagining he'd slighted people when nothing of the sort had occurred. I said, 'My mum's cool with it. And so's my dad.'

There was silence for a bit. I put my arm around his shoulder, not caring whether the people who walked by on the path a little way behind us saw us or not. Or what they might think if they did. And he – it wasn't only me who was the copycat – put his arm round me.

I said, a propos of nothing – or everything – 'Remember the last time we sat like this? On the jetty at Lazise?' It was hardly likely he'd have forgotten. It was the first time we'd said, *Ti amo*. I was being rhetorical again. 'That song came into my mind,' I said, in answer to his silent nod. 'The Schubert one. In the Schöne Müllerin. One of the ones we didn't sing.'

To my great surprise he started singing it. Not *bel canto*, or *can belto*, but almost under his breath, the way a mother sings to her child. *Wir sassen so traulich beisammen im kühlen Erlen dach.* We sat so snug together in the cool of the alder trees' shade.

How had he known which one of the dozen songs we hadn't done I'd meant? I was startled to hear my own weedy untrained voice chime in with the next line... *'Wir schauten so traulich zusammen hinab in der rieselden Bach.'* We looked down so close together, at the mill stream running beneath.

I felt Michele clasp me tighter in his surprise. 'Oh hey,' he whispered. 'Oh hey.' And then somehow we carried on through the song together. An Italian boy and an English one singing in German together with not very good accents. A man with a future as an operatic tenor, and another one, with a ho-hum voice. We sang to each other together, almost under our breaths. And when one forgot the words a moment, the other would carry him on.

The tune is by Schubert. Heine wrote the German words. The English ones are mainly mine.

The moon was out, and brightly.
The stars gleamed out beyond.
And looked so right together
In the silvery mirror pond.
But I saw no moon in the mirror,
I didn't see the stars.
Hers was the face I saw there,
I saw no stars but her eyes.
I saw her nodding and smiling

As ripples fretted the stream.
Her eyes were like the forget-me-nots
That smiled on the banks of the stream.
Then deep in the water below us
The whole of heaven spread,
As if it wanted to draw me
Into its watery bed.
While over the stars and the moon's face
The little book raced on.
It seemed to say in its murmur,
'Come join me, lad, let us be one.'
Da gingen die Augen mir über,
Da ward es im Spiegel so kraus.
Sie sprach: es kommt ein Regen,
Ade, ich gehe nach Haus.
My eyes filled up with water,
The mirror distorted and bent.
She said: it's starting to rain now.
I think it's time I went.

We stopped. The song had ended. We didn't try to look at each other. Michele squeezed me with his arm most tenderly. 'I never heard you sing before,' he said. He sounded choked.

'I can't sing properly,' I answered him in a wisp of a voice.

'You sing well enough for me,' he said. 'You sing more beautifully than anybody else.'

'But you're not going to get up and go now, are you?' I asked him. Trying, pretending to be light about things. 'Even if I do drop tears into the lake.'

'No, I'm not,' he said. Then he wriggled slightly in our side-by-side embrace. 'I'm not sure how to tell you this. I had a text from Valentino earlier.'

The change of gear shocked me. It was like getting out of fifth and accidentally hammering into first. 'Who's Valentino?' I asked him. Who the fuck is Valentino was what I meant.

'He's the boy I was in love with at university. The one I was staying with last week.'

'I know,' I said abruptly. 'The one you had a *sega* with on our lawn.'

'Don't say that in that tone of voice.' Michele now sounded distressed. 'He wants to come and stay for a few days.'

'I see,' I said. 'And you said...?'

'He's having trouble with a few things. He needs someone to talk things through with. I said, yes, OK.' He stopped. We still had an arm each around the other, and we could feel what the other was thinking very clearly: the puzzlement and the hurt. 'Is that all right with you?' he finished, sounding timid now.

I think it's time I went. I didn't repeat the last line of the song back to him although I thought it. There was silence, an awful silence for a minute or more, while we both tried to adjust our thoughts. We didn't take our arms away from each other's shoulder, though. Then, tentatively I put my head against his and kissed him. And tears that came from the eyes of both of us dropped into the lake.

TWELVE

Monday morning. Back to work. But compare this Monday morning of mine with most other Monday mornings you can think of. We were going sailing, the three of us. Sandro, Michele and I. We would sail out from Garda in the sunshine, across the lake to Sirmione. We'd have lunch there and sail back. I'd teach Sandro a few new words and expressions, and maybe learn to sail a boat. I'd be with the younger, smaller boy I fancied, and the slightly older, slightly bigger one whom I also fancied and with whom I'd fallen heavily in love. And he with me, of course. As Oh-hell-it's-Monday mornings went... Well, it could have been worse.

We chugged down the shore to Garda in the tiny motor boat. Tied it up in the harbour, and transferred to the Luccini's yacht.

It was a cool piece of kit. You steered with a wheel, not a tiller, and it was thoroughly well equipped. It had radio and radar, and GPS. Not that we'd need those today. We could see the wooded high ground of Sirmione quite clearly, about eight miles distant across the lake.

I watched, and tried to help, as we steered out into open water, using the engine (yes, it even had one of those) and the brothers set and trimmed the sails. I tried to find the vocab for it all. I knew there were stays and shrouds and sheets, but I wasn't sure which were which. Damn. I should have looked it all up on the internet last night, I thought. Then, never mind. It could be a task for Sandro and me one day when we were working indoors.

We headed back the way we'd come, though further off shore this time. Sirmione was south-south-west of us – that showed up very exactly on the GPS – and so we saw the Luccini's house, and later the Punta San Vigilio, recede, bathed in sunshine, a long way to our right.

This morning we were all three of us in shorts. It might be breezy out in the centre of Lake Garda, but the temperature was hot. The wind was blowing warmly from off the land-mass of the Veneto to the west.

I said to Sandro as we blew steadily along our route, ''Chele's got a friend coming in a few days. Valentino. Did you meet him?' Perhaps this was naughty of me. Michele and I hadn't referred to Valentino again after our little shower of tears the previous afternoon at the water's edge. I thought that bringing the subject up in Sandro's company might defuse things. Or be the controlled explosion, under expert supervision, of a ticking bomb.

'Yes, I met him,' Sandro said, after a moment's hesitation during which he glanced quickly at his brother's face. 'I thought he was nice.' A pause. 'Handsome also. I thought ... as we seem to be getting quite open about this subject these days ... that he was gay but that he didn't want to be. Couldn't admit it to himself.' He looked at Michele in a slightly challenging way and said – I think that before yesterday he wouldn't have done this – 'And you had a big thing about him, 'Chele. I realised that.'

'How do you know that?' said Michele. He sounded

slightly shocked.

'It was obvious, 'Chele,' Sandro said, laughing. 'You're not the poker player that you sometimes think.' Michele had the grace to smile at that. Of course he did. One thing he always had was grace. Sandro had more to say on the subject, though. He'd assumed the role of my big brother a few days ago, and hadn't got hurt, and now, perhaps emboldened by that experience, took the same role upon himself in regard to Michele. 'Be careful, 'Chele. You might find yourself bringing the embers of a dead fire back to life when Valentino stays here. You can't let that happen, though. You've got Hen to think about.'

Michele looked for a second as though he'd been slapped, rather than spoken to very lovingly by his brother. Love is sometimes tough like that. But he recovered himself very quickly and said simply, quietly, 'Thank you for that.'

It wasn't for me to say anything at that point. But I'd been deeply moved by Sandro's concern for me, and by his courage in voicing it at the risk of his brother's wrath. And he'd referred to me as Hen, without asking my permission, but simply because he'd heard Michele call me that. He did it because he knew I'd like it. I had liked it, of course.

I changed the subject. I thought it was about time one of us did. 'Words with WR,' I said. 'How many can you get?'

'Wrangler jeans,' Sandro suggested.

'Good,' I said.

It took a little while to get going, but then the words

came quite fast. 'Wriggle,' suggested Michele, then explained to Sandro what it meant. Despite the ergonomic difficulties presented by our being in a sailing boat, he wrote it down at once. Bless. Then he himself came up with wrestle, and sounded pleased with himself.

I reminded them of wrist, and then wring...

'Wring, wrung, wrung,' shouted Sandro jubilantly. He still hadn't forgotten those irregular verbs.

'Wrought iron,' I told them. 'And wreath.'

Sandro didn't need a prompt from me this time. 'They're all about turning and twisting,' he said, sounding delighted with his perspicacity.

'Yes,' I said. 'So what do you call a car that's a twisted heap of metal?'

'A wreck,' the brothers both said.

I had done a little bit of homework. I'd flicked through that page of the dictionary before setting out. So I was able to give them wraith, and wrath, and wrap and wrench. And wrinkly and writhe. Even wrong, which took a bit of thinking about. I didn't trouble them with the bird called wryneck, a woodpecker with a habit of twisting its head. 'There's another very easy one,' I said. 'It's about looping and curving, and you do it by moving your wrist about.'

Sandro came up with a word, but it didn't have an R in it, and so was disqualified. I said, 'it's the verb, to write.'

*

The village of Sirmione is one of the treasures of the lake. A village that is almost an island, approached from the land by a three mile natural causeway. I'd seen it from the aeroplane as we came into land, and described it earlier as looking, from the air, like a chameleon's darting tongue. Approaching over the water, of course, you don't see it quite like that. But arriving from the western side of the lake as we were doing involved quite a big circle around the head of the peninsula, as the harbour and village centre were on the other side.

I couldn't help noticing its affinity with Venice. The Venetians had once ruled the towns and villages of the lake, and had brought their fairytale architecture here. Houses with filigree mouldings, windows with ogee curves and Gothic tracery. And those festive looking mooring posts around the harbour that look like many-coloured barbers' poles.

As soon as we'd tied up Michele had an urgent phone call to make. He'd been unable to do it earlier: there'd been no signal while we crossed the lake, and he'd thought it too early in the day to do it before we left home. He called the number Signor Grippi had given him and was given an appointment to sing for him at six in the evening on Thursday. Just three days away.

Towards the end of the phone-call I heard Michele say something – in Italian, of course – that I rather hoped I'd misunderstood. He didn't leave me in suspense for long though. As soon as the call was ended he turned to me and said, 'I asked if I could bring my own accompanist. They said yes.'

'Your own accompanist?' That alarmed me. Did he mean...?

'I meant you, of course.'

'Oh God,' I said. 'I'll have to pull my socks up.'

To my surprise it was Sandro who answered. 'That's a nice expression: pull your socks up. But you don't need to. I heard you accompanying him when you rehearsed together over the weekend. You do him justice fully.' Then he wrote *pull your socks up* in his book.

The trouble with spots that are famous for their prettiness is that everybody goes to them. The little streets of Sirmione heaved with people. You could hardly move. Tourists of every nationality thronged the roadways; every single one of them seemed to be demolishing bright-coloured ice-creams in cones as they walked. And most of them were rather big. It was like the bull run in Pamplona, only with big people instead of bulls.

We peered through the door of café after café but in none of them was there an empty seat. In the end we bought takeaway beers and pizza slices, and ate them standing in the street.

Like everybody else.

Everything was indeed very pretty. But only if you started looking at things more than six feet off the ground. We fled the streets eventually and walked along the forested tip of the peninsula that we had earlier circled in the boat. There was an olive grove, in which bone-white Roman ruins stood and lay about. It was supposed to have been a villa lived in by Catullus. Everything seemed to be connected to Catullus in these parts.

And after our walk, we returned to the harbour, hoisted our sails and trimmed them, and set off for home.

It took longer on the way back. The wind was pretty much against us, and we tacked long zigzags back and forth. Who cared? We had the company we wanted. At least I did. Sandro might have been missing Daniela, but if he was, he never said.

I was finding it difficult to keep my hands off 'Chele, and I know from the way he looked at me from time to time that the same went for him. But out of respect for Sandro – and his parents, come to that – I resisted the temptation. I was being paid to teach him English, after all, not to grope his brother in a boat. Even so, we touched each other often – and Sandro too – as we moved around the rocking cockpit deck every time we changed tack.

Sandro said, 'I've been thinking about wriggle, writhe and wrestle, and wondering which ones applied to you when I found you both on Saturday. Because you weren't just wanking, were you. You were having a proper fuck.'

'Sandro,' said Michele in an outraged tone, 'Can you leave it? It's a private thing. You weren't supposed to be there.'

'It wasn't private at all,' Sandro objected. 'You were doing it on a public footpath. I was walking along the same public footpath, where I had every right to be. If you'd wanted nobody to see you, you should have chosen somewhere else.'

Michele didn't really have an answer to that. Instead, I volunteered the information his little brother seemed to be after. 'If you must know, Sandro, we each fucked the other. Michele went first, then I did him afterwards. I'd just finished coming when you spotted us.' I'd thought, let him just have the whole thing, or he'd be chipping at it for the rest of the sail back.

'Oh wow,' he said. He sounded quite excited by what I'd told him. And for a straight boy, rather eyebrow-raisingly so. For he didn't just sound excited. I looked at his shorts – I couldn't help it, he was standing up, at that moment in charge of the helm – and there was a little ridge in them, pointing to four o'clock.

That set off a chain reaction, I'm afraid. My dick was nothing if not a copycat. And Michele, seeing what was going on in my shorts, soon found a partial erection in his.

Sandro had a further observation to share with us. 'I didn't know two guys could do it facing each other,' he said. 'I thought you had to do it like the animals. You know, one on the other's back.'

'You can do it that way,' I volunteered. I was the only one of us, after all, who had ever done that. But, Heavens, I thought. What a topic for an English lesson! Whatever would his parents say if they found out? Nevertheless I continued. 'But it's nice face to face. Especially if the other guy's got a handsome one, and even better if you're both in love.'

'Doesn't sound too bad, actually,' said Sandro a bit thoughtfully. 'Like doing it with a girl almost. In fact it sounds quite nice.'

Dear Sandro, I thought. Whatever are you saying? I had to restrain myself from doing what I wanted to just then: reaching out and grabbing the thing, now in ten o'clock position, that was tenting up his shorts.

Michele took charge then, thank Goodness. He said, 'I think it's time to change the subject. No?'

So we talked of other things. None of us wanted to be the first to mention that trio of erections – it would have been awkward and embarrassing, and a bit of a minefield: two lovers and the brother of one of them... And so none of us commented on them, even jocularly. But all three of them stayed up for most of the rest of that zigzag journey back across the lake.

*

There would be no drinking in lakeside bars for Michele and me that evening, nor for the following two nights. We had to work on his audition songs. We had decided, after much discussion, not to repeat La donna e mobile. 'He's heard you sing it already,' I told Michele. 'Don't waste one of your songs on something he's already heard and liked.' So we settled on Una furtiva lagrima, from Donizetti's L'elisir d'amore, and – from Puccini's La Bohème – Che gelida manina: the words usually rendered in English as *Your tiny hand is frozen.*

'And then give him a German Lied,' I'd told him 'Show him the gentle side of your voice.'

'Really?' he said.

'Yes, really,' I insisted. He followed my suggestion, and we started to work on the last but one of the Schöne Müllerin songs – The Miller and the Brook. It was wonderful to have my advice followed meekly, for the first time in my whole life, by a slightly older guy with whom I was in love. It was so wonderful, in fact, that I stopped worrying about whether my advice was right.

That Monday evening we worked together at the piano till nearly ten o'clock. When we stopped, and I got up from the piano stool, Michele said, 'You sang so beautifully to me yesterday. Would you do me a favour and sing that song for me again?' Rain of Tears it was called. In German, *Thränenregen.*

'What?' I thought he must be joking.

'Please. Sing it for me. I'll do my best with the piano part.' Then he sat down on the piano stool, a place I'd never seen him sit before and didn't at all associate with him, and leaf through the score until he found the page.

'No way. I couldn't,' I protested.

'You did it yesterday,' he said.

'But you sang it along with me. We just marked it. There was nobody to hear us...'

'Your voice is beautiful,' he said.

'But your parents are in the house. They'll think we're crazy...'

'It's OK,' he said smoothly. 'If you sing it in German they won't know what the words mean.' He was wilfully misunderstanding what I'd meant.

Calmly Michele began to play the piano introduction. He played the right notes with confidence and conviction, at the correct, steady, lilting pace. It took me back to the moment he'd jumped into the water and I'd followed him in. It looked like I had no choice.

'Wir sassen so traulich beisammen...' I began. It came out in a breathy voice that managed to be both under-powered and rough. Like someone who has never done it before drawing a bow across a violin. Michele didn't stop. As I struggled miserably on into the second phrase I heard Michele humming softly along under me. I felt that soft touch of his voice beneath mine, beginning to bear me up, like a father's big hand beneath the tummy of a child who is learning to swim.

I felt my voice grow stronger. Michele's humming stopped. I was singing on my own now. I finished the first verse.

'That was good,' I heard 'Chele murmur, as he played the intro to verse two. 'Go on,' he said, and then, 'Towards, towards.'

The acoustic in that room was lovely. I'd reckoned without that. And then I heard something I'd never heard before. My voice was taking wing. It began to fly during the second verse, then soared on into verse three. As he played the intro to the fourth and final verse, which moves into the minor key, Michele slowed the tempo a little. The effect of that was magical. And it nearly broke my heart.

The words came to an end. I sang my final note. Michele went on and played the last five plaintive bars that belong to the piano alone. I stood where I was behind him, still looking over his shoulder at the music, rooted to the spot. Then he got up and turned to me. We hugged as we'd never hugged before. 'You lovely man,' he whispered. We were both overcome. Over his shoulder I saw his mother open, and then softly close the door.

THIRTEEN

There was the question of what we'd wear. It was to be a fairly informal audition, we guessed, at the end of a long day of rehearsal for Signor Grippi. And the weather was really hotting up that week, which was another consideration. Sandro said that Michele should sing dressed in no more than a wet towel around the waist and freshly watered hair. That way at least they'd remember who he was.

Some good sense underlay Sandro's facetious suggestion. We decided in the end, and Sandro agreed with us, that we would wear the same clothes we'd had on the day of the 'rescue'. Nearly identical khaki cargo shorts and sky-blue short-sleeved tops. (All washed and ironed since Saturday's escapades, you'll be relieved to hear.) That would make us look as close to twins as we were capable of looking, with our different features and complexions. That might not help Michele in his aim, but it would surely touch the heart of even the toughest judge: this demonstration that we were a team. Not just good partners in music but two boys who were clearly very much in love. And it would serve Sandro's very serious purpose. To remind Grippi not only who we were, but that, wearing these very clothes, we had plunged into water to rescue him and his friend.

On the other hand, however much we wanted to look like twins in Grippi's eyes, the same would not go for Michele's mother. She was keenly interested in what he was going to wear, and when he told her, after a bit of reflection, gave her blessing to the idea.

She was also interested in what I was going to wear. I'm afraid I lied to her. I said, chinos and a plain white shirt. I would have to leave the house in those, and change en route for Vicenza, in the car.

I hadn't told Michele about his mother opening the door on us while we were locked in an embrace by the piano that night. Had she wanted to make a scene at the time she would have done so. Instead, she'd softly withdrawn and closed the door. She hadn't referred to the incident since. At least, she hadn't said anything to Michele or me.

I told Sandro the story. He was my confidante now and my treasured friend. I asked him if he thought I should tell Michele. He said, 'For God's sake wait until after the audition. Then tell him anything you like, or else don't.' Sometimes he was wisdom personified.

I said, 'Has she said anything to you?'

He said, no, not yet, but that he'd tell me if and when she did. 'She may not have known that you saw her,' he added. We left it at that.

Those last days before the audition passed in a bit of a blur. I spent more time on my own with Sandro during the hours I was supposed to be teaching him, though Michele was never out of our thoughts. If Sandro and I were in the house or garden, or even on the shore of the lake, we'd hear him trying over phrases in the piano room, occasionally playing a snatch of the accompaniment for himself. Once we heard his voice, pursuing us through the open French windows, across the lawns, the shore, the water, when we were a little way out on the lake in the boat.

The sound, the experience of that, was wonderful. I

caught Sandro looking across at me strangely. 'Hey, oh hey,' he said. 'He's made you cry, I think.'

I said, 'He does that rather a lot.' I brushed at my eyes with my knuckles and smiled. Then, to my utter surprise, Sandro got up from the gunwale opposite me, leaned across and kissed my cheek.

I told Michele about that incident that evening, when we were rehearsing after dinner. When we finished for the night Michele, who had obviously stored it at the back of his mind while we'd been working, said, 'Do you know that song by Schubert: To Be Sung Over the Water?'

I did. He said, 'Do you want to do it with me? Now? Just for fun?'

I was still sitting at the piano. I said yes, and began to leaf through his book of Schubert songs. He said, 'No. I'll play it. You do the words.' He wanted me to sing.

I hadn't done so since that time two nights before. I said I'd try. I got up and let Michele sit down. The song isn't difficult for the singer. It doesn't go too high and the intervals lie comfortably within the capabilities of an untrained tenor voice. But the piano part, while not difficult, has a lot of notes. I wondered how good Michele's sight-reading was. 'Have you played it before?' I asked him as he found the page.

'Yes,' he answered. 'A friend at Padua liked to sing it. I played it for him.'

I didn't ask, but I hoped the friend was not Valentino.

Michele launched into the intro. All those quick little

notes; they represented the ripples on the lake's surface. He managed them beautifully. I couldn't have done better myself.

When it came to my entry – well, Michele would have done *that* better, much better. But even so, I didn't think I was too bad.

'Out on the mirror-like, shimmering waters, gliding like swan goes the ripple-rocked boat...' But I did it in German, which sounds a bit more butch. We did all the verses, then stopped.

There was no wild embrace this time. We just looked at each other. Michele looked at me with something like pride. I looked at him – I imagine – with an expression that said, *Did I do OK? I think perhaps I did.* I can only guess at the expression on my own face, but those were certainly my thoughts.

'You may never make the windows rattle,' Michele said. 'But you've just given a lovely encore to all the people down by the lake tonight. The lovers on the shore. The people out in boats...'

'Oh my God,' I said. I'd given no thought to the fact that the doors and windows were still open to the cooling night. And if I'd heard Michele's glorious arias from the lake earlier that day, then my much inferior offering had been presented in the same way just now to whoever was out there in my place.

Michele said gently. 'Just believe me. Have faith in yourself. You have a fine, serviceable voice.' He got up from the piano and poured us a whisky nightcap. We took it outside with us and sat on the bench under the cedar tree. A figure emerged from the darkness, preceded by the sombre red glow of a small cigar. It was Signor Luccini. 'Was that Henry I heard singing just now?' he asked. I made a sort of Mmm noise in my throat. Michele said, 'Yes it was.'

'He sings very nicely for an English boy,' he said. 'Michele is very lucky in his choice of friends.' He said nothing else, but passed on into the house.

Michele and I looked at each other and squeezed hands. We were both wondering the same thing, and didn't need to say it out loud. Had Michele's father, in a rather coded way, given us his blessing? Had we just been given – as it were – a blessing in disguise?

A few minutes later came the muffled sound of voices talking. People were walking up the garden from the door in the wall that led from the lake. Sandro and Daniela. Michele called to them a moment later and they came over to where we sat.

'Who was that, singing the last song?' Daniela asked, though there could hardly have been much doubt.

'That was Henry,' Michele told her. 'What did you think of his voice?'

'Gentle and soft,' she said in Italian. 'We thought it was lovely. We were out in the boat.' She stopped, then giggled, then turned to me. 'You made Sandro cry.'

*

We went to Michele's room together, as we always did now, though we were still discreet about opening doors and the noise we might make. Our thoughts were full of the morrow's audition. I wondered how we would sleep.

As we entered the room and Michele turned on the light we both saw a piece of paper on Michele's – our – pillow. It was a handwritten note. He picked it up and read it. Then, without comment he passed it to me. It was in Italian. It was from his mother. It read, very approximately, as follows.

My darling son

Tomorrow will be a special day for you. We shall all be thinking of you when six o'clock comes. Be frightened of nothing and all will go well.

His mother had signed it simply with her first name.

But the note continued after that. On the same piece of paper. I read it dumbstruck.

Henry. You have been a wonderful support for 'Chele. Look after him well tomorrow, and cherish him in the time to come.

It was some seconds before either of us could speak. The ramifications of that note, a note to both of us on the same piece of paper, and left for us both to find on Michele's pillow, our most intimate and private place, were vast.

I found my voice first. 'Bloody hell, Michele,' I said.

*

I was given a day off from teaching Sandro. Nevertheless, he spent most of the morning with Michele and me, in the garden and in the house. Together we managed to stop Michele rehearsing too much. 'Just a little,' I said, 'from time to time throughout the day.'

Michele grew more nervous as the day wore on, though he tried not to show it. I was nervous too. Nervous for him, and for myself. OK, my piano playing wasn't going to be judged. It would barely be listened to. But I still had to get it right and, by giving Michele good support, give him confidence too. I remembered how his soft humming had supported my faltering voice a few days before, and given me strength. This afternoon my piano playing would have to do the same for Michele too.

To get to Vicenza we would take the motorway past Verona and then about twice as far again the other side. It would take about an hour. After he'd unlocked the Aventador, Michele stopped and looked across at me rather searchingly as I stood, about to climb into the passenger seat on the other side. 'You know what, Hen?' he said. 'I'm a bit tensed up. I don't feel like driving. Would you mind...?'

And so I found myself, for the first time in my life, bombing down the *autostrada* at the wheel of a Lamborghini sports car...

We found a public car-park near the Teatro Olimpico, where, before walking to the theatre, I changed my clothes. Despite the evidence of her bedtime note last night I was still not sure that Michele's mother would have wanted me to go on-stage looking like a darker, slightly smaller, copy of her son. So the plan had not been altered. I wore long trousers and a white shirt, and only got into my shorts and blue top when we arrived.

The Teatro Olimpico in Vicenza is the oldest indoor theatre in Europe. It was built by Palladio along soaring classical lines that are guaranteed to put the wind up any auditionee who walks towards it. By the time we reached its portico we felt about mouse-size.

We announced ourselves at the ticket desk. At least Michele did. We were a few minutes early, he said, but he had an audition with...

'And I'm a few minutes ahead of schedule too, unusually,' said a voice behind us. We turned. Signor Grippi, in open-necked shirt and jeans. 'But if you're ready we can make a start.' He gave us each a smile. Then he put a hand on Michele's shoulder. 'I'm glad you've chosen that relaxed way to dress. Though I'd have remembered you anyway. Just let the relaxed feeling extend to your voice. Remember, it's only an audition. It's only me. You're not having to dive into cold water now.'

He led us along corridors to the backstage region, and showed us onto the stage. A rehearsal piano, a small grand, was being wheeled in from the wings on the other side by two men. 'Just give me time to take a seat,' said Grippi, 'then start as soon as you're ready.' I sat down at the piano in readiness and peered into the vast auditorium.

It wasn't only Grippi, of course. The friend who'd gone boating with him was dimly discernible, sitting in the stalls, and with him – and joined a minute later by Grippi himself – were two other people, presumably senior members of the opera management, a woman and a man.

Grippi called again, 'When you're ready.' I looked at

Michele. He looked at me. 'Towards, towards,' I said to him. He nodded. We began.

To say it went well would have been an understatement. Hearing Michele's voice fill that huge space gloriously was like nothing I'd ever heard before. I'd heard him in the open air, and in his parents' drawing-room. Was my playing inspiring him to such heights? I didn't know. I knew that his singing was inspiring me.

He did the Donizetti first. One furtive tear. Then the Puccini. Your tiny hand... Finally Schubert. The Miller and the Brook. Well, I had no idea if Michele had managed to impress the expert panel out in the stalls, but he had mightily impressed me.

I heard Grippi call out. 'Thank you. Now would you like to come down and talk to us?' Michele gave me a look as he began to walk away from me towards the wings. I can't describe it, though you probably know it anyway. I stayed where I was, sitting on the piano stool, waiting to be told where to go.

Then I heard Grippi's voice again. 'You too, Mr Henry. I want to talk to both of you.'

Arrived in the stalls we sat awkwardly in seats in the row in front of the panel, twisting our heads and bodies around in order to look them in the face.

'Michele,' Grippi began. 'If I had a vacancy for a tenor starting tomorrow morning, or next week, I would hire you tonight. You sang very splendidly just now. But I don't have a vacancy, as I told you, and for now, I'm sorry but that is that. However, I won't forget you. And I'm glad you didn't think it necessary to jog my memory by coming along tonight clad in a towel.

You will be hearing from me one day with an offer of work. That is a promise. The bad news is simply that, at the moment, I can't tell you when.'

It was about as good as we could have hoped. Michele beamed and looked relieved.

Then the woman on the panel addressed me. 'How long have you known those piano parts?'

I said, 'Since Saturday.'

I saw her do a quick mental count. 'Five days.' Then she said, 'Can you read from a full orchestral score?'

'I've only really attempted it once or twice,' I told her.

She picked up a big book from the seat beside her. 'Could you read this?'

I wasn't quite sure where this was going. I only knew that once again I had to jump in with both feet. I opened a page at random. I just saw squillions of dots. 'I could try,' I said.

'Then try,' she said. 'Show me what you can do.' And she gestured back the way I'd come, towards the stage and the lonely place upon it where the piano awaited me like a bull awaiting its matador.

It was Rigoletto. Thank God I knew how it went. I struggled through the pages of La donna è mobile, grabbing the fistfuls of notes I could reach, and leaving the others out. But keeping the time going come what might. When I'd finished I thought I was going to faint.

I heard her call out to me. 'Well done. Now come

back down.' There was a sheen of laughter on her voice.

She told me her name and introduced herself. She was the chief repetiteur for the company. 'My assistant is leaving in the autumn,' she told me quite matter-of-factly. 'I'll need a new rehearsal pianist then. Would you be interested in the post?'

Oh God, I thought. I don't know about this. I'm not ready for that. Not up to it. The autumn... What would have happened between Michele and me before then? There were too many things to think about. 'Can I have time to think it over?' I heard myself asking amidst the whirlwind of my thoughts.

At once I heard Michele's voice, just inches from my ear, saying very firmly, 'No, Hen, you can't do that. For God's sake just say yes.'

FOURTEEN

We went to Venice. It was by way of celebrating the outcome of the audition. Michele's audition. And what had turned out to be mine. Sandro came too, of course. It was a teaching day, and this was one of his lessons.

Rather than drive all the way, and deal with the nightmare of queueing up for parking when we got there, we took the train. Emilio – that was the name of the chauffeur butler – took us to the station at Peschera. The train did all the rest.

It took us through Verona and Vicenza. It gave us views of mountains where I hadn't expected them. It took us through Padua, which had been Michele's home for the last three years and would be Daniela's home for the next three, while Sandro studied in Rome. I wondered what the transport links between the two cities were like.

And then it showed us Venice from across the water, like something in a fairytale. It must have looked even more romantic a century or so ago, before they built the bridge, when all arrivals were necessarily by boat, and you entered the city via the Cannaregio canal. But even to arrive the way we did, by train along the bridge and into the vast train-shed of the station was pretty good.

Michele and Sandro knew how to deal with the ticket machines for the water-buses, and were the focus of attention, while they sorted them out, for the swarms of tourists who did not.

I'd seen pictures of Venice. Who hasn't? But nothing

prepares you for the real thing. Even to step out of the station onto the waterfront of the Grand Canal was like walking into a dream. We took the vaporetto number one and slid further and further into it.

Palaces everywhere, and every building a palace. An array of colours, all different, quite random, like the little boxes of water colours in an artist's paintbox. Big windows, small windows, oriels and lancets, gleaming in the sun. All looked fresh and lively whether they'd been cleaned recently or not.

All the palaces had water doors. Some a prudent foot or two above the level of the water, others whose bottom sills were invisible beneath it. Some were smartly painted and well maintained, others had been rotted by the waves or gashed by boats. Every bend we turned opened onto a new and glorious prospect, swinging into view over open bright water as if conjured. I had to remind myself to breathe. No wonder gondoliers sang.

At each stop a stout rope was slipped over the head of a mooring-post and held there for a moment while people got on and off. It was as fleeting as a stop held on the foot-brake... And then we were off again, while new arrivals swayed and tottered towards seats. We disembarked at St Mark's Square, threaded our way between tents that sold every kind of tourist bric-a-brac, and once we'd reached that famous open space, were promptly set upon by doves.

'How long do you think before they offer 'Chele a job?' Sandro asked.

How long was a piece of string? I taught him the expression there and then. 'I really have no idea,' I said. 'Maybe months, maybe a year or more. At least the offer has been made.'

'There's nothing in writing, though,' Sandro said. That was true. There was nothing in writing for me either, yet, although there would be soon. I'd been promised the paperwork would come by post.

Needless to say I couldn't help feeling awkward about this. We'd gone to Vicenza with a view to getting Michele a foot on the ladder towards a career in opera, yet it was I that had ended up with a definite job and he had not. But he had been wonderful about it. When, in bed last night, I'd told him about my uncomfortable feelings on the subject he'd said, 'A job for you is a job for me. It's a job for us. There is a thing, now, called us.' A minute after that, this new thing called *us* had made love.

The cool interior of St Mark's Basilica. Mosaics twinkling in the half light. The paintings by Tintoretto and Veronese in the sumptuous state rooms of the Doge's Palace. The baroque frontages by Sanmichele and Sansovino around the square... It was a bit like eating six dinners at once. Eventually we plunged into the cool shade of an alleyway and went in search of a pizza by way of a respite.

'There was an English writer called L.P.Hartley,' I told the other two. 'He's most remembered now because he wrote the book, The Go-Between, which was turned into a film. Anyway, he was gay, and lost his virginity to a gondolier in the bottom of a gondola.'

'Either he must have been very rich, or it was a long time ago,' said Sandro. 'It would cost a fortune now.'

Michele and I looked at each other and burst out

laughing. Michele said to his brother, 'And how would you know that, little one?'

Sandro was unabashed. 'Because everything involving gondolas and gondoliers costs a bloody bomb. Stands to reason.' Costs a bloody bomb. I was glad I'd taught him that. It always pleases a teacher to see his efforts produce results.

'I think it was the 1920s,' I said. 'Though it might have been before the First World War. I'm not too certain of his dates. Anyway, I think it'd be fun to have sex in a gondola,' I went on. 'Something to put on one's CV.' We were eating a pizza at a table in an alleyway, under a sunshade. Two girls at the next table turned and looked at us, giggled and turned away again. It's easy to forget that English is understood everywhere.

'I'm not sure how we could manage that,' said Michele, speaking a bit more quietly than I had done.

'We could steal one,' said Sandro. 'Pole it out into an empty bit of the lagoon. You could do it there.'

'With you watching us?' Michele said. 'Again...? No thanks!'

'Oh, I don't know,' said Sandro with a cheeky laugh. 'I might want to join in.'

'That's called incest,' I said. 'It's not allowed.'

'It wouldn't be incest if I restricted my attentions to you, Hen,' Sandro said, and looked me very challengingly in the eye.

'Then it would be something else,' I said, and

laughed, to show I was making a joke of it. At least, I think I was. 'It's called infidelity. Me to Michele, you to Daniela. And also,' I added for good measure, 'you're not supposed to do it with your brother's spouse. I've forgotten what the name of that is. It's in the bible, anyway.'

'Bugger the bible,' Sandro said.

I looked deep into his eyes then. I was a bit ashamed of my reaction to what I saw there. I started getting hard. The human body is like that. That's the way we're made.

Michele looked at us. He gave a half laugh and said, 'Stop it, you two.' In just the same amused tone of voice that Sandro had used to reprove him and me on the boat back from Gardone just nine days ago.

*

Venice is quite hilly. Did you know that? Well, I'm exaggerating of course. It's not hilly like San Francisco is hilly, or even Edinburgh. But I'd imagined the pavement level would be like the terrace outside the Houses of Parliament in London: spirit-level straight; at all points the same height above the Thames. Instead I found the alleyways undulated gently, rising and falling in some places by a metre or more.

I asked Michele why this was. Was it because richer people centuries ago had been able to afford to raise the levels of the ground they lived on, with a view to reducing the risk of flooding to their homes? Or because of subsidence over the hundreds of years since the city had been built?

Michele said he had no idea, and that he'd never

thought about it before. He said it was great to go to a familiar place with someone who was new to it. You saw it anew for yourself through their eyes. 'I'm also seeing it with the eyes of a man in love for the first time in my life,' he added.

I said, 'So am I.' For a moment I found myself dreading that Sandro might say something wildly inappropriate at this point, but he did not, for which I was glad.

But he did say, a little while later, as we mooched through the labyrinth of little streets, 'You could always do it in an alleyway, I suppose. In a doorway or up against a wall, while I kept guard.'

The idea had a massive appeal at that moment. I looked at Michele and could see from both his face and his shorts that the idea appealed to him too.

But it was broad daylight and even the deepest, darkest, most crevice-like alleyways were lit by the ricocheting rays of the sun this July afternoon. 'We'd have to come back at night, I think,' said Michele.

All the same, we found ourselves looking hopefully at doorways we passed, or nooks and corners between the walls. And although there weren't people in sight at every moment, a figure or two would always appear around a corner, or out of the entrance to a house, just when you weren't expecting it.

'Sex in Venice,' said Michele musingly. 'It sounds like the title of a film.' It did sort of ring a bell with me too. I wondered if perhaps it had already been done.

We got lost of course. Michele told me that was part of the place's charm. Everyone got lost in Venice, he said. Even people like himself and Sandro, who had been here lots of times. We'd see light at the end of an alleyway, and make towards it, only to find it shone through a wire-mesh fence, with the waters of the Grand Canal, its be-ribboned gondolas, and its whooshing water-buses, on the other side.

But just as you can get lost easily, so you can get unlost almost equally easily, in the same way you find you've suddenly sorted out a tangle in a length of string without knowing how you did it. Suddenly we were on familiar ground. It was familiar to the two Italians at any rate. We found ourselves at the back of the old fish market near the Rialto bridge.

We climbed the stone steps inside of the bridge and I thought (like every tourist who climbs that bridge and has done The Merchant at school) *Signor Antonio, many a time and oft in the Rialto you have rated me,* and then wondered – along with all the others – what came next.

'Be fun to do it here,' I suggested light-heartedly. 'In the middle of all this lot.' I meant the crowd.

'And be arrested, and in all the newspapers in Italy,' Michele said.

'Arrested in Venice,' said Sandro. 'It sounds like the title of another film.'

Personally, I thought the idea of being in all the newspapers in Italy, for whatever reason, was not half-bad.

*

In the end we didn't get to have sex in Venice that

day. We had a late supper in Peschera after we got off the train. Dinner-time at the Luccini's house had come and gone. We phoned Emilio, he came and found us, and drove us home.

Then Sandro went off to be with Daniela. While Michele and I...

We sauntered down to the bottom of the garden, where the little motor boat lay just inside the gate in the wall. We took a pair of oars with us this time, dragging them as well as the boat out through the gate and into the water. It was dark as well as late, and we didn't want to sully the lakeside peace with engine noise.

We rowed out a little way into the lake, then stopped, and shipped the oars. I think that's the right word. It's what I told Michele we were doing anyway. And then we just sat there and listened to the late evening sounds.

We could hear the calls of people on the waterfront at Garda village, half a mile away. Across the shining black water we could see the lights of all the bars and ice-cream parlours there. The floodlit front of the Loggia della Losa, and of the other Venetian building nearby, that stands in Piazza Catullo alongside the Piccolo Hotel.

Nearer at hand came little splishes in the darkness. Michele said that was fish. Then another little splashing sound and a quack. That wasn't fish but a brood of ducklings out for a late night adventure with their mum.

'We could pretend we are in a gondola,' said Michele.

I said, 'I was wondering how long it would be before one of us said that.'

We were sitting facing each other, me on the plank across the stern from which the engine and tiller were worked, he on the rower's plank amidships. He came towards me in the motion of someone slipping off their seat in church and onto their knees. He managed to loosen the fastening of his shorts at the same time, so that by the time he came to rest, kneeling in front of me, the tops of his thighs were bare and his cock was jutting forward in front of him, wagging like an eager puppy's tail. Though the tail of a pretty hefty puppy, it would have had to be. 'I think this has been coming on all day,' I said.

Michele lifted up his T-shirt and pulled it over his head, throwing it into the bottom of the boat. Then he did the same to my T-shirt; I raised my arms in the air to help him do it. Then, because there was nothing left on me except deck shoes, he went for the waistband of my shorts. I half stood for the next bit, so that he could get them down below my knees. I was conscious of the fact that the last time we'd seen two men do anything remotely ambitious in a boat as small as this one they had overturned it and both fallen out. But I reckoned that if we both stayed astride the centre line of the keel we'd be OK. I hoped for the best, at any rate.

Once I was sitting back down again Michele pulled my shorts right off, then, shifting his weight off one knee after the other, did the same with his own pair. Except for deck shoes we were now stark naked, under the stars, in a small boat out on Lake Garda and alone except for the fish and the ducks.

Michele took my erect penis into his mouth.

No, it wasn't the first time this had been done to me. But it was the first time Michele had done it to me. I felt very honoured. It was a very special treat.

He took in the whole length of it easily. Took it in his stride, you might say, if only that didn't muddle the image a bit too much. I didn't know if I'd manage his so easily when my turn came. Assuming it did...

Actually, I began to think it might not come as soon as all that. Michele, kneeling and bowing in front of me as he sucked and licked me, had one hand down in between his own legs and was feverishly beating himself off.

Well, you know me well by know, so you know what the next thing was. I felt my cock getting ready to come. I told Michele this, so he'd have a chance to remove his lips from me if he didn't want to get my come in his mouth.

He didn't answer me, obviously, but he didn't remove his lips. So I spurted into him and he drank me down without any sign of surprise or that he wasn't liking it. I've already said he was graceful in everything he did, in every move he made. Well, he even did that with grace.

And a moment later he came, of course, coaxed by his own rapid hand. All over my left shin – I felt its molten-lead spatter – and down along the keel-line of the boat.

FIFTEEN

Signora Luccini had said nothing to either of us about the note she'd put on Michele's pillow and that had so astonished us. She had gone on behaving towards us, together and separately, exactly as before. So we weren't quite sure now how we were supposed to behave in return. Were we to be an openly gay couple in the house, publicly throwing arms around each other, and kissing every time our paths crossed in the hallway, whether anyone was looking or not? Saying goodnight to the family at bedtime and walking upstairs together, brazenly going into 'Chele's room?

Actually, we had no idea how openly gay couples did behave in their parents' houses or anywhere else. Neither of us had been here before. We'd never before been *us*.

So we went on exactly as we'd done until now. We continued our bedtime pantomime of opening and closing doors on the landing, and we didn't hug or kiss in front of the rest of the family. It seemed the most sensible approach. Nor did we make a point of dressing alike. Although, strangely enough, that seemed to happen of its own accord, again and again.

My contract and other papers arrived from Opera Vicenza in the post. Enclosed in the package were the tickets that Grippi had promised us for Rigoletto the following week. Not just two of them, but six. We telephoned him to say thank you. It seemed weird. In the autumn he would be my boss, and at some unknown date in the future, Michele's also. We'd be working together in rehearsals, Michele and I. That also was a strange thought.

We spent our days out on the lake mostly. Michele, Sandro and I. Sometimes we sailed in the yacht, sometimes, more lazily, we took the public boats – Mantua, Verona and the others. Either way, we'd end up at one of the nearer lakeside villages for lunch. Bardolino, Lazise, Gargnano...

In the evenings 'Chele and I would do Schubert songs just for fun. There was no urgent need to rehearse opera just for the moment. Sometimes Michele would take over the piano stool and get me to sing. They were nearly all love songs, of course... Later, when Sandro was out with Daniela, we would wander down to the village and drink a beer or two at one of the bars. And one night that week we again rowed the little boat out into the lake when it was quite dark, and we pretended we were in a gondola again, stripped naked, and in a role reversal of what had happened after we'd come back from Venice, I took 'Chele in my mouth and after a while he came down my throat, in a very lover-like way.

*

Then things changed a bit. Daniela went away on holiday with her parents and sisters. It was the last family holiday before she went off to university. Who knew what would happen then? It might be the last family holiday she'd ever take with them.

Sandro said, 'University changes things. It changes everything. You know how many boy-girl relationships that begin at school survive the first year at uni? I looked it up on the web. It's about zero percent.'

I said, 'with boy-boy relationships it's even less than that. I don't need to look that up.'

With Daniela's departure Sandro found his evenings suddenly devoid of purpose. In the daytime of course it was Michele who tagged along with him and me, joining in – and actually learning a bit from – Sandro's English course. Now, on the day that Daniela disappeared, when Michele and I decided to go down to the Loggia della Losa after dinner, it was Sandro who asked diffidently if he might tag along with us. 'You did teach me the expression, to be a gooseberry. So I don't want...'

'It's fine,' I said, after exchanging an all-clear signal with Michele in the form of two almost invisible nods. 'We love your company,' I said, speaking for the pair of us. It was better to do it that way. I was beginning to think I loved Sandro's company a bit too much, given that I was totally in love with someone else. I hadn't known that particular little trick that love can play on lovers before this summer. Now suddenly I did.

It was fun to be walking down the lakeside path towards the village as a trio. To see and smell the roses and the jasmine as we passed. It wasn't as though Michele and I were having no time together, after all. We had hours of each other's undivided attention, and each other's hearts and cocks, in bed together every night.

'Three beers,' Michele ordered when we got there. He did it in English, either absent-mindedly or as a joke. And then he laughed, and looked at me. 'Remember Two Beers?' he said.

'Oh my God, yes,' I said, and laughed. It seemed a

world away and an age ago.

Sandro laughed too. 'Yes, I remember Two Beers. That was your first night.' He looked at me and narrowed his eyes a little. 'Because I know you better than I did back then, I'll ask you this. Did you have sex with him?'

'Yes.' I left it at that. I left it to Sandro.

'I thought so,' he said triumphantly. 'But how – where did you manage that?'

'Against the wall on the lakeside,' I said. 'We walked past the spot just now.' I saw Sandro's eyes flick towards his brother, questioning, but also protectively. I loved him for doing that. 'It's OK,' I said. 'Michele knows all about it.'

'My God,' Sandro said. 'Gay boys are so immediate. No? Your first day here it's Two Beers, the second day Michele.'

'It's been Michele ever since,' I carefully pointed out. 'But yes, it can happen like that.' Sandro turned away from us suddenly and looked out over the darkening lake. I tried to read his thoughts by staring at the tousled waves of the back of his head. Without success.

A minute or so later he was back with us. 'What are we all going to do when Valentino gets here tomorrow?' he asked. It was a question that had been much on my mind, though I hadn't had the balls to voice it. Apparently Sandro had. 'Will he join us on our English lesson jaunts?'

'He's very welcome to if he wants to,' I got in before

Michele had a chance to speak. I wanted to make it as easy for him as possible.

'I don't know,' 'Chele said. There's something he wants to talk to me about. I don't know what. But that won't take four days. We can find out what he wants to do. He might enjoy practising his English with all of us. Who knows.'

'Play it by ear,' I said.

Out on the lake a flotilla of ducklings was bobbing on the residual waves that were left over each evening after the passing, all day long of the big boats. (By morning, ten hours after the boats had ceased to ply across the lake and before they started up again, the water would be as smooth as a glass of milk.) We had noticed this particular duck family over the last couple of days, because one of the ducklings stood out, being a different colour from its brown and beige striped siblings. It was bright yellow all over and would, we all guessed, be white when it grew up. But there is a price to be paid for standing out in a crowd, and this evening the little yellow duckling would pay it with its life.

Black kites regularly patrolled the waterfront, about a hundred yards off shore and a hundred or so feet up. To and fro they'd go all day, roving between the two tree-clad outcrops of rock that bookended the village. They were a gorgeous sight. We sort of knew what they lived on, but tried not to think about it too much.

'God, look!' Michele said suddenly, and pointed out over the lake. A kite was in mid-swoop towards the water, down towards the ducks. Within a second it had grabbed the yellow duckling, scooped it off the surface of the lake and was bearing it aloft. We saw it, tucked under the hawk's tail like a bright pom-pom.

But already the most amazing thing was happening. The mother duck had taken off in pursuit and was following the kite into the sky, quacking her heartbreak. She stood no chance, her speed was barely half that of the kite, though she flew fast enough. The kite became a speck in the evening sky while the duck was still at fifty feet. She had her other ducklings to protect. At last she turned, and circled back in to land among the remainder of her brood.

I hadn't known before that moment that birds had hearts. And that they could be broken, just like ours.

For a second we sat in stunned amazement, not looking at one another. I felt a terrible ache in my chest. And then Sandro started crying. Softly at first, and then in an unstoppable flood, and with loud sobs that everyone at the nearby tables would have heard. He was sitting on my left, Michele on my right. 'Chele now got up quickly, went round in front of me to his brother and wrapped him in his arms as he must have done when he was a kid, while Sandro went on weeping quietly on 'Chele's neck.

*

There was an atmosphere of tense expectation next day. We were all acutely conscious that Valentino would be arriving at the end of the afternoon. We knew that there would be all kinds of complications connected with that, though none of us knew exactly what they would be. None of us wanted to talk about it, it seemed, and so we talked of other things. We took a break from boating that day, though not from the lake. We walked to Bardolino, along the curvaceous shoreline. Through the whole of Garda village and out the other side and then two miles. Although the day was baking hot the path was shaded along much of its length by lines of willow and poplar trees, and a cooling breeze blew through them from the sun-dazzled lake.

Bardolino is famous for its light red table wine, which is rather sweet. Many people find it really lovely and it's very famous all over the world. My own verdict? I think I'll pass on that. We arrived there around lunchtime and parked ourselves outside Da Rimaldì, where we ordered crab frittata and, braving the frowns of our waiter, a carafe of cold white wine from somewhere else.

We spent our afternoon ambling slowly back.

'FL,' I said.

'Foreign language,' Sandro fired back, quick as a squaddie to the salute. 'TEFL: Teaching English as a.'

'Well done you,' I said. 'But I didn't mean that. I meant words beginning with.'

'Flat,' said Michele.

'Hmm,' I said. It wasn't one of the ones I'd been thinking of. 'I meant verbs,' I said.

'Fly,' said Sandro. That was better, but it brought back memories of the mother duck last night. We saw that in one another's faces.

'Flow,' said Michele, equally unfortunately. We all immediately thought of Sandro's tears. But it began to get better after that.

'Flee,' Sandro said.

'Flutter,' said Michele, sounding very pleased with himself. 'Like in the Strauss operetta. The Bat. *Die Fledermaus*. The flutter-mouse.'

'It's actually flittermouse,' I said. 'That's the old English word for bat. Butterflies flutter and bats flitter. There's no argument about that.'

'Flood,' said Sandro.

'And flourish,' said Michele, unwilling to be outdone.

I gave them float and flounder. And fling and flicker and flick.

Then Sandro said, 'I've cracked it. They're all about moving things through fluids...'

Michele chipped in. 'Or fluids moving themselves.'

'And it's all to do with the vowels again,' said Sandro. 'The dark ones are for movement in liquids: float, flood, flounder. The bright ones – fly and flitter – are about the air.'

'And it's about the speed of movement?' Michele suggested a bit shyly. 'Bright vowels for fast – flee – and dark ones for slow?'

'I think you're both right,' I said, with impartial generosity. 'Which is why butterflies flutter and bats flitter, and why planes fly and rivers flow.'

I wasn't going to be an English teacher for much

longer. I thought I ought to enjoy it while I still could.

Valentino arrived, driving his own car, a Porsche, with impeccable timing, a few minutes before cocktails were due to be served. I'd seen pictures, I think, of Rudolph Valentino, a matinee idol of a few generations ago. I'd imagined, perhaps lazily, that Valentino who was coming to visit, whom Michele had fallen in love with, and who had wanked Michele off on the lawn, would be similarly tall, dark and handsome, with old-style matinee idol good looks.

The reality was quite unlike that. He had good looks certainly, but was small – smaller than Sandro – blond, delicate-featured and petite. He had big round blue eyes like a doll's, and a little, snubby, slightly turned-up nose. I didn't blame Micehele for having fallen for him once. I thought he was dead cute.

He was also charming. He made a point of coming and talking to me over cocktails. I was the only person there he hadn't previously met. 'Do we talk English or Italian?' he asked me.

I said, 'Your English sounds as good as Michele's. My Italian's not so hot. I never get a chance to practise it though. So it doesn't get better.'

He smiled, and said in Italian, 'Then have a little practice now, with me.'

And so we made a little small-talk. He went slowly, and was patient with me, not using slang but always the correct words. We talked about the weather, and about his car and his drive down here this afternoon from the Dolomites. And all the time I was asking myself questions about him in my head. Questions that I was far too well-mannered to have asked someone I'd only just been introduced to, but which intrigued me nonetheless.

For example, what was he doing here? What was it that was so much on his mind that he needed to drive down and talk about it with Michele? That he couldn't simply deal with in a text, or an email, or a friendly discussion over the phone?

I became aware that I was not the only one of us who was hiding other thoughts behind the trite Italian sentences we exchanged. I saw in his nice blue eyes that he was trying to form opinions, judgements and ideas about me. I liked him for that, though. And I was fairly confident that he liked me too.

It was over dinner that I got my answer. (Spaghetti with clams and mussels, Venetian style. Calves liver with marsala sauce...) He sat opposite Michele. I sat two places away. Whenever Michele was speaking Valentino hung on his words, and when Michele looked in any other direction, or addressed someone else, he followed him surreptitiously with his eyes. Perhaps he didn't even know he was doing it.

And I knew then what Valentino had come to talk about with Michele. He'd come to tell him that he'd lied to himself, and to Michele, for years and years. He'd come to tell Michele that he loved him. And that, despite all his previous protestations, he was gay.

SIXTEEN

I hadn't really been on my own with Sandro since the days before the audition, when Michele was up to his ears in practising his songs. But Valentino's arrival changed things. Michele told me at breakfast what I already knew. That he wouldn't be joining us this morning because he and Valentino were going for a walk. That Valentino had told him he needed a bit of time alone with him because he needed to talk...

I said, 'Yeah, yeah, I know all that.' I smiled at him and added, 'I'm fine with that. Don't worry. See you later, and we can catch up.' Michele then gave me a look: a lovely, wonderful look ... that hurt us both.

I'd known since last night what Valentino wanted to talk about, though I hadn't said anything to Michele about it when we were in bed. We'd had better things to do, and talk about. I wondered now if he knew what he was in for. I'd have to wait until this evening to find out.

Sandro and I took the boat out and chugged across the little bay, which was fresh and morning-smooth. I looked for the traces of my emissions and Michele's on the planking under my feet but the dew of the last couple of mornings had cleaned it all up. We steered into Garda village harbour and tied up.

We hopped onto one of the big boats. It didn't much matter which one, or where she was bound. It happened to be the Solferino, and she was heading for Limone, at the northern end of the lake.

I was getting used to this. And loving it. Gliding like

a swan (thank you Schubert, thank you, Heine) past the garden wall of the Luccinis' house. Rounding the tip of the Punta San Vigilio and turning, this time, sharp right. There was the little harbour where 'Chele and I had jumped into the water. People were already seated at the tables there. Little matchstick folk at this distance. Having coffee, I supposed, because it was a bit early for wine or beer. Little did those good people know what dramas had unfolded there ten days earlier. They couldn't know that two gilded youths had plunged into the water, like Icarus in duplicate, and that one of them, a future opera star, had astounded all who sat there by singing from Rigoletto, clad in only a towel...

We were sitting, Sandro and I, in our favourite seats, on the open deck in the Solferino's bow. Sandro chose that particular moment to press his knee against mine. We were both in shorts, so it was his flesh against my flesh. Warm, and bony as all knees are, yet soft. 'Don't do this, Sandro,' I said.

Did I say that? Like fuck I did. I returned the gesture with my own knee, and pressed his knee back.

They're not the most beautiful bits of the body, knees. They're an awkward hiatus between the charm of someone's calves and the glory of his thighs. But they're a true indicator of whether you love someone or not. I loved Michele's knees because they were Michele's. I now found that I loved Sandro's knees because they were Sandro's.

It became like arm-wrestling. A kind of arm-wrestle of the legs. Neither of us spoke. We just increased the pressure, both of us, till we could almost feel the skin of our knees burning. Our legs stayed exactly where they were, moving neither towards the right (Sandro) or left. (Me.) We used so much muscle power, both of us, that we nearly went blue in the face.

Our little ship began to turn to starboard, towards its next port of call. Torri del Benaco. Approaching it across the water, you couldn't wish for a prettier sight. There remained the question, though, of what to do about Sandro's knee. The only answer I could think of was to put my hand on it. So I did.

He turned to look at me, and gave me a cautious smile. He reduced the pressure he was exerting against my knee, thank God, and I relaxed mine against his. I said, 'We mustn't do this, Sandro. You've Daniela to think about, and I've Michele.' My tone of voice didn't sound too convincing. I didn't even convince myself. I left my hand where it was. If the other passengers wanted to look they would see it. If they wanted to be shocked they could.

Sandro looked ahead of him, at the view of Torri, pretty as a postcard, where we were now tying up. He said, 'I read stories in the papers sometimes. About school-kids or university students who fall for their teacher. Silly girls, mostly. Occasionally a boy who likes the idea of an older woman to show him things he didn't know. Things to do with the body. Things to do with the heart. And every time I've thought, how stupid. How stupid. How fucking stupid can you get?'

He stopped, and the silence that followed was very long and big.

Eventually I said, 'Sandro...' And then I stopped. I hadn't the remotest clue what I could say next. I gave his knee a little squeeze instead.

In full view of anyone who cared to watch us he crossed his arm over mine and stroked the inside of my bare thigh, running his fingers a little way up inside my shorts.

It was wonderful, of course it was wonderful. I'd thought he was wonderful the moment I met him. I'd thought about him, fantasised about something like this happening between us, that very first night. And despite the wank I'd had with Tobias on the beach path, I'd masturbated, thinking about Sandro, when I got in bed.

I took my hand off his knee and used it to remove his hand from my thigh. I placed that very gently on his own knee, in the place where mine had just been. I said, 'Sorry, Sandro. We have to stop.'

He knew the truth of that. He didn't look at me, so I couldn't read that knowledge in his eyes. I clocked it from his body somehow. Not from any movement he made. He didn't move at all. But somehow there it was. It was like I had access to his heart.

I surprised him with a question. 'Why is might sometimes right?' I asked

'Might is right, sometimes... Hmm, let's see.' He sounded relieved to be playing a language game. So was I in a way. What I really wanted to do was to smother him with kisses. And I felt complimented beyond all imagining, knowing that he wanted to do the same to me. 'Ah,' he said. 'You're not talking about might, meaning strength or force. You mean the modal verb.'

'Correct,' I said.

'So why's it sometimes right? Give up,' he said.

'People have stopped using it,' I said. 'Even journalists and novelists. They use may all the time instead.'

'Right,' he said, and nodded his head. We were approaching our next stop, which was Malcesine. The approach to Malcesine over water says to the visitor, 'You thought Torri was pretty. Now take a look at me.' With its battlemented towers – the battlements in the shape of kites' forked tails – and snow-capped mountains as its backdrop, the shining water in front of it...

'But it's about degrees of certainty, no?'

'Sure,' I said. 'And sometimes it matters very much. What about 'Hitler may have invaded Britain in 1940'?

'Wrong,' said Sandro. 'That sounds as though we don't know if he did or not. And of course we know he didn't.'

'Exactly,' I said. 'He didn't, but he might have done.'

We went on discussing the intricate subtleties of modal verbs and all their finer points as we made our stately way up the eastern shore of the lake. It narrowed gradually, and the mountains on either side of it rose higher, and more sheer out of the lake, until it seemed we were navigating our way up a Norwegian fjord. Then we crossed over to the western shore and to Limone, where we disembarked.

Limone, as its name might hint to you, is a place that's famous for growing lemons. The village, pretty and stone built, is as if set on a giant flight of steps that ascends the mountainside. The three or four bottom steps are streets of houses. Above, the buildings give way to terraced lemon groves. I saw that nets were suspended above each terrace. Sandro told me they were to protect the lemon trees from the winter frosts which rolled down like cold stair-carpets from the mountains above.

Then Sandro said, 'I need to go pipi.' I did too, as it happened. There was nobody about. So beside the low stone wall that raised the lemon trees above the path we both unzipped our shorts.

It was a moment that was of major importance for both of us that day, yet one we didn't attempt to speak about. Our first sight, each of us, of the other's cock. We were both half hard by this time. Sandro was in all respects a size or two smaller than I was, and that went also for his dick. It was, however, perfectly in proportion with the rest of him, and one of the prettiest I'd ever seen in my life. I was sorry when, after he'd accomplished what he'd set out to do, he put it away again. And from the look on his face he was sorry when I stowed mine away, after shaking it, and zipped back up.

'We'd better go back down the hill,' I said, 'And look for something to eat.'

*

We had – guess what? – a pizza and a glass of beer. Eating, we sat facing each other across a restaurant table. It was the first time we'd really had to eyeball each other since breakfast, as we'd been walking side by side, obviously, and had sat side by side on the boat. We studied each other's faces carefully. The complex nature of the things we read there were too difficult to find words for. Too difficult even to contemplate.

Strolling in Limone's streets afterwards, killing the time before the return boat, Sandro suddenly put his arm around my shoulder. He felt my slight shock of surprise, and said, 'Don't think about it. Straight Italian males do this all the time.'

'Yes,' I said, and then, without thinking, 'But we're not straight Italian males.' I realised at once the implication of what I'd said, but it was impossible to withdraw the remark. I waited for Sandro to say something – anything – but he said nothing. He kept his arm around my shoulder, though, and gave me a little squeeze. I put my arm around his shoulder then, and we continued to walk Limone's streets like that, like drunken sailors, I thought, until it was time to catch our boat.

The Verona took us back. As we headed out across the narrow northern end of the lake, the Punta San Vigilio came into view almost at once. It still looked like a crocodile's head, even from this side. Though, at a distance of nearly twenty miles it was very much a baby crocodile.

Again we sat on that little triangle of deck in the bow that we liked, on very close-together seats. *Wir sassen so traulich beissamen,* I remembered from the song. We sat so snug together. Yes, but that line was supposed to be Michele and me, not me and Sandro...

Ach, Bächlein, aber weisst du wie Liebe tut? Oh mill-stream, dear old mill-stream, dost thou know what love does?

It plays the strangest tricks.

'What are Michele and Valentino doing, do you suppose?' I asked. Really simply to make conversation. At once I realised how unwise this was, and wanted to kick myself.

Because Sandro said, of course, 'Probably much the same as us,' and, leaning in to me a bit, laid the whole of his forearm along my upper leg.

'Sandro, don't,' I pleaded, in a voice that came with a threat of tears. But I meant that and didn't mean it at the same time, of course. I wanted his hand there more than anything at that moment, whatever the risk of capsize to Michele and myself. I don't know who coined the phrase, *a standing cock hath no conscience,* but he deserves to be better known, whoever he was.

I leaned in to him slightly as I laid my arm carefully over his arm, and interlocked my fingers with his. My head was now touching his head, my short dark hair mingling with his longer, sun-warmed black locks.

He said, 'Look what you've made me do.' I looked in the obvious place, and saw the hard-on tenting his shorts and the wet spot at its tip. Before I had time to look down at my own crotch he said, *'Et tu, Brute.* We're bad boys both.'

Sandro, this must stop *now*, I wanted to say, but the words didn't want to come out. But then Sandro's whole body tensed and went rigid. 'Ah, no!' he said. I knew what had happened to him without even looking. Nor did he need to tell me, but he did anyway, in a shaky, shaken whisper. 'Shit. I've just shot in my shorts.'

I didn't have time to say anything to calm or reassure him. To my utter shock and horror I suddenly did the same myself.

*

We were dry by the time we got home, at least, though our shorts looked a bit on the grubby side. We met up with Michele and Valentino at cocktail time.

People know somehow, don't they? I've never quite worked out how. Michele kept looking at me and then at Sandro, and then back again. We talked about how our day had been, of course, though we left certain bits out. But I couldn't help noticing one or two things myself. The looks that Valentino kept shooting towards Michele were different from yesterday's, and not so easy to read. And Michele's shorts, which had been clean on that morning had – like mine and Sandro's – a somewhat used look about them now.

The four of us went down to the village together. Valentino drove us in his car. We sat on the lakeside, drinking Veneziano cocktails just for the hell of it, trapping the setting sun in them just before it went down. We talked of safe and silly subjects, rather boringly. I wasn't alone with Michele until we got to bed.

Then he held me very close to him and whispered, 'I can live with it if the answer's yes, but did you have sex with Sandro? I really need to know.'

It's not always as clear cut as all that, the question of whether you've had sex with someone or not. An American president famously got tangled up in the semantics of that once. I said, 'I don't think so.'

'You don't think so?' He laughed as he said that, so it could have been worse, I thought.

'We held hands on the boat a bit,' I said, 'and accidentally got a bit overwrought. We also – again accidentally – then both came in our shorts.'

'I see,' said Michele thoughtfully, though he never stopped stroking me.

'Your brother's gay,' I told him. 'At least, he was today.'

'I think I've always known that,' said 'Chele. 'It's one of those things that brothers somehow know.'

'And Valentino?' I hazarded. 'Since we're on the subject. Did you have sex with him? After what I've just told you, I can hardly object if you did.'

Michele sighed. 'A bit yes and no, if you can handle that idea. Much like you and Sandro.'

'I somehow guessed that,' I said. 'Just as you guessed about Sandro and me.'

'Valentino's gay, you know,' Michele said. 'That's one of the things he came all this way to tell me.'

I said I knew that. That I'd worked that out last night.

'The other thing is that he's in love with me, unfortunately.'

I said I knew that too.

'Maybe,' he said slowly, thoughtfully, 'it might be

an idea if we spent the day together tomorrow, all four of us.'

I agreed. We spent a little longer discussing things before we went to sleep. We seemed to be in agreement. Things could have been worse. The fact was that we hadn't had sex with anyone else, either of us. It was just that we might have done.

SEVENTEEN

Valentino was quite keen to come on an English-speaking boat trip the next day. Well, Michele was coming too, so he'd be bound to be keen, really. I did feel obliged to run the idea past Signora Luccini after breakfast – carefully choosing the moment just after her husband had left for work. I didn't want to be accused after the event of spending time that I was being paid to devote to Sandro with other people. There was already Michele coming along with us wherever we went – except for yesterday, and look at the consequences of that! – and now there would be four of us. Which was quite a number, considering I'd been hired for a one-on-one course.

But the boys' mother said yes, that would be fine. Valentino was only here for a few days, and it was only natural that he'd want to spend his time with us other young folk. She clearly didn't see the situation, as others might have done, as that of Valentino improving his English at her and her husband's expense.

In fact there was a kind of wisdom about her that I couldn't help admiring. She was far from ancient: still in her mid-forties. Yet she seemed to see through to the depths of things, but almost without knowing that was what she was doing. I'm not quite sure what the best word for this is. Insightful? Perspicacious? Intuitive? Prescient? That famous note on the pillow, to which none of us had ever referred since, was pretty strong evidence of this quality. Whatever the word might be.

We walked down to the village. The little boat would have been a bit of a crush with four of us on board. Then we got the service boat – this time to Gargnano, on the other side of the lake, a little way north, and roughly midway between Gardone and Limone. All of us except Valentino must have been turning over memories of those two trips. I know I was. Especially as the boat was the Verona, which had been involved on both those other occasions, either going or coming back. The weather was a little cooler today; the fierce temperatures of the last week had dropped off. For this reason we had all set out in long trousers rather than shorts. I did reflect on one possible unintended consequence of this. It might – though only might – help us all to keep our hands off each other on the boat.

Valentino was a fun addition to the group. And his English was up there with Sandro's. He asked if we could practise past conditional sentences at one point, and Sandro – whose lesson it was – was quite happy about this. So we played a kind of chain game of consequences. Things like... *If they hadn't jumped into the water, they wouldn't have pulled Grippi out. If they hadn't pulled Grippi out, he wouldn't have auditioned 'Chele. If he hadn't auditioned 'Chele....* etc. etc. *And we wouldn't have tickets for the opera tomorrow night.* This game nearly always ends up in the present. In which respect it's quite like life.

The lake villages seem to compete quite deliberately for your favour as to which is the prettiest. Yesterday we'd seen Torri and Malcesine from the water, and had walked around Limone. I'd thought them all lovely. As to which I preferred, the jury was still out. There were Sirmione and our home village of Garda to consider too. And now, across the water, and slowly drawing nearer to us, its rooftops glinting in the sun, Gargnano appeared, and was at least as lovely as the rest.

We walked round the cool interior of the San Francesco church, and paid attention to the carved capitals in the cloisters there. Sculpted citrus fruit of all kinds. The Franciscans had introduced them to the region centuries before. Coming out of the church and walking down the street nearby we saw a cone of white apparently hanging weightless in the sky: a mountain peak so far distant that all it showed of itself was its summit snow.

Sandro got a text from Daniela, on holiday in Sardinia. 'She's met someone who's going up to university at Padua when she does,' he said. In a splendidly neutral tone.

Hmm, I thought. 'Girl or boy?' I asked.

'Boy,' he said. 'He's going to study politics, same as she is. They'll be in the same faculty.' I thought Hmm again.

On the boat back (Trento this time) we had to sit two and two. I next to Michele, while Sandro and Valentino were in front of us, twisting their heads towards us as we talked. Because of his smallish stature Valentino looked young for his twenty-one years. Almost a match for Sandro. I couldn't help thinking that they made a pretty pair.

I had been sharing with Michele over the last few days my anxiety about my new autumn job. Reading all day long from orchestral full scores. Was I really up to it? Crashing through a bit of Rigoletto the other day to impress the lady repetiteur in Verona had been one thing, but I'd had very little experience of it before.

'You only get good at something by doing it,' Michele had told me. We agreed I'd need to get hold of opera scores and practise reading them during the next few weeks. Perhaps the opera company would lend me some. It would be in their own interest after all.

Now suddenly, midway back to Garda on board the Trento, Michele remembered something. 'There's a full score of Rigoletto somewhere at home,' he said out of the blue. 'In the attic, I think. You could have a go at reading that.'

There was still an hour to fill before cocktail time when we got back home. Michele found the score after a bit of searching. It was a hundred-years-old edition, ragged at the edges and yellowing a bit with age. But it was clear enough to read ... albeit difficult for me to play.

'I'll help you,' said Michele. 'Or stand behind you at any rate, and give you moral support.'

There wasn't time to do the whole thing before dinner, obviously, but we did the whole of Act Three. Michele did more than stand behind me. He sang the arias and dialogues of the Duke of Mantua, the tenor part he'd done when at university – including of course La donna è mobile – and hummed or sang most of all the other parts under his breath. Somehow his presence there and his singing got me through this labour of Hercules. Though I was ready for my cocktail afterwards, I can tell you.

*

Next day the four of us went for a sail in the yacht. Valentino was almost as much of a novice as I was, but we all had fun. We didn't go far. Lessons were finishing early, as we were going out in the evening. Lessons is a dull old word for what we were actually doing: talking English together while sailing a boat. Especially when everybody seemed to be rather complicatedly in love with everybody else. And yet we were learning so much, all of us. Including me.

I taught the others the words of Uncle Tom Cobley, and Old Macdonald had a farm, and On Ilkley Moor baht 'at, and we sang them as we sailed. And if you've never heard the sound of three Italians singing On Ilkley Moor baht 'at in cod Yorkshire accents … well, I can tell you, you've missed a treat.

We changed out of our wet clothes and smartened ourselves up at the end of the afternoon. We had a light, early meal. There were six tickets and six of us were going: The Luccini brothers and their parents, Valentino and me. It needed two cars to get us to Verona. 'Babbo' drove his wife and Sandro and Valentino, while Michele, at the wheel of the Aventador, took me.

I had seen the outside of the Roman Arena when we'd gone to Verona, although we hadn't been inside. It had looked, I thought, like the Colosseum in Rome, and seemed to be about the same size.

Inside it was, well, colossal. The open air venue, big as a football stadium, seated fifteen thousand, Michele said. Around us stone benches rose in tier after tier. A giant horseshoe shape whose acoustics were famous throughout the world. Until the previous year, opera had been sung there without any backup in the form of microphones. We didn't sit on the stone benches, though thousands did. Signor Grippi had looked after us well, and we were shown to red upholstered seats in the centre, on the flat, in the stalls.

A note was handed to us. It was from Grippi himself. He wouldn't be in the house for the first two acts of the opera, but hoped to be around towards the end, and would try to say hallo to us afterwards.

The opera began in daylight, but it would be dark by the end. The stage would be floodlit and the audience given candles to hold.

It was true that the acoustic was a marvel. Every voice rang out like a bell. Whenever the Duke of Mantua appeared I could see Michele, sitting next to me, mouthing his words. Well, he'd sung the role himself in Padua, and had sung the final act as recently as yesterday afternoon. It seemed he still knew the whole thing by heart.

The drama unfolded, in a way I can only describe as seeming effortless. I had the feeling that the words and music had cost no effort to write. That the period costumes had appeared by magic. That no effort had been expended by the singers in learning and rehearsing their roles, their words, their moves. What I was witnessing was an example of 'the art that conceals art'. The business of being professional rather than amateur, in other words. And a frisson of nervousness and excitement ran down my spine at the thought that I'd be part of this process, part of the company, sitting at a piano with them during rehearsal in a few weeks' time. Working with these very men and women whose voices were now – so effortlessly it seemed – filling this enormous, sky-open space.

So it went through the whole of Act One and on into Act Two. But then in the middle of the second act I began to notice something. I thought that the voice of the tenor playing the Duke was showing signs of strain. Though I wasn't sure. I whispered to Michele, 'Is he having a bit of trouble, do you think?'

'I think he may be,' Michele whispered back.

Towards the end of Act Two there was no doubt about it. The man was struggling in the cooling evening air. The sun had gone behind the high wall of the Arena now, but was lighting the oval sky above us with burnished blue and gold. Little by little, so subtly that you were hardly aware of it, the stage lighting came to life. While, little by little, the voice of the poor singer who played the Duke began to die.

Small seeds of light began to scatter here and there among the high stone tiers. The audience was beginning to light its candles up. Then Act Two finished and there was thunderous applause and noise.

An usher appeared at the end of our row. 'Signor Michele Luccini?' he queried hesitantly. Michele identified himself. 'Would you come with me, please, sir?' the usher said. 'Signor Grippi would like to see you backstage. If you're agreeable he has a little job for you.'

Michele and I swapped glances. His was one of terror and shock. We knew that he wasn't being summoned just to set a few props or sweep the stage. 'Oh God, Hen,' he said. 'Is this what I think it is? It can't be.'

'You sang the whole of the third act yesterday,' I reminded him. I tried to sound calm and reassuring, but my voice trembled as I spoke. 'You did it with me.'

'That was in a drawing-room,' he said. His voice became little more than a whimper then. He said, 'I'll be too small.'

I said, 'Just do it like yesterday. Just sing for me.'

'Then hold my candle,' he said, a bit more sturdily. We'd both just lit them. Now he handed his to me.

'Signor Luccini...' said the usher in the gangway.

'I'm coming,' he said. He began to walk along the row. His mother, then his father, then Sandro and Valentino all touched his hand for a half second as he passed them. He reached the gangway. He turned and looked at me the way he'd done after his audition in Vicenza. Then he was led away.

I sat holding on to the two candles: the one I was holding for Michele and the one I was holding just for me. I held them as tight as if my life depended on my doing so. I held especially tightly to the one that was Michele's. I knew that I wanted to hold onto it for ever now.

*

The interval dragged on a bit. The audience began to talk and move its feet in a restive sort of way. The way people do when they think some sort of announcement is imminent, but don't yet know what it's going to be.

Then the announcement came, over speakers that were very loud. Owing to the sudden indisposition of the singer playing the Duke of Mantua, the part would be taken over, during the third and final act, by Michele Luccini, who had very kindly agreed to step in and sing the remainder of the role. Because of the short notice and for other practical reasons which it was hoped the audience would appreciate, he would not be appearing in period costume but in his own clothes.

'And with a book to read the words from, I should hope,' his father said. I thought, maybe, maybe.

The orchestra struck up the curtain music for the third act. A world in miniature bustled onto the stage. Then, looking very far away and rather tiny, Michele himself appeared.

He was wearing pale fawn chinos and a cobalt blue silk shirt that, by chance, exactly matched at that moment the shade of the not quite dark sky.

I knew of course how the act began. It begins with the Duke launching into La donna è mobile. 'Chele took a pace forward – he was carrying no book – and launched into it.

He was nervous. Horribly nervous. I could tell. I think everyone else could too. He began the aria perfectly in tune, but his voice sounded unsure of itself, a little boxed-up for the first line or two. I remembered what he had done for me a week or two back, and now I did it for him. I began to hum along with him, under my breath. A father's hand supporting his kid's tummy as he begins to swim. Of course he couldn't hear me. I doubt if even Sandro next to me could hear. But I willed Michele to get my message. I whispered, 'Towards, towards.'

And little by little his voice came to him, like a great engine that has been reluctant to start, stuttering its way to soaring life.

Of course I'd never heard him sing better. I'd never heard him sing in a Roman theatre before, with an acoustic to die for and an audience of fifteen thousand. His voice came strong and beautiful. Liquid as the lake we'd left that day, grand as the great sky above.

The stars were appearing one by one. *Look how the floor of heaven is thick inlaid with patines of bright gold.* And how the tiers of the Arena were inlaid with thousand on thousand of tiny candle flames. I held my own candle tightly still, resting the foot of it on my knee. 'Chele's I held even tighter, resting it on my other knee. Then I felt something. Sandro's hand had slipped onto my hand. He wrapped his fingers around his brother's candle too. I looked down, then along the row. I saw Sandro reach out with his other hand to the candle Valentino was holding. A bit diffidently Valentino reached and held 'Chele's mother's light, and then she completed the chain by taking hold of Babbo's. I saw him give his wife a peck on the cheek just then. And so we all sat there, linked by our hands and by little flames, linked by the love we all bore Michele in our different ways while, a long way in front of us, and no longer looking small, he sang his great heart out, and quaked the night air.

EIGHTEEN

The next morning we were in the newspapers all across Italy. Well, of course Michele was. But *we?*

After the end of the show Grippi had taken us – the six of us – to a small place he knew where you could get a late-night bowl of pasta and a glass of wine. A few other members of the opera company had come as well. Everyone was full of 'Chele's performance and his talent and wanted to celebrate with him and congratulate him. We also wanted, I think, to bask a little in the glory that had radiated out from that moment of his. For he'd been blooded that night. He'd not only been a credit to himself and to Grippi's confidence in him, he'd become a professional singer at a stroke.

He was also about to become quite famous as well. We weren't alone with our pasta and wine for long. Men with cameras, and women too, were everywhere. Like fruit-flies when you uncork a bottle. You wonder what they were doing before.

The whole story came out. Not least because of Sandro. Michele and I might have held back from telling the story of our dive into the water at Punta San Vigilio. Grippi would almost certainly have refrained from telling the press how he and his partner had been rescued from four feet of water because one of them had flipped a small boat while trying to tie it up. But Sandro had no hesitation in spilling the whole can of beans. The auditioning of the towel-wearing Michele on the harbour-side. The unlooked-for bestowal of a job as a rehearsal pianist on me... And who was I exactly? Sandro's English teacher, and Michele's friend. The faces of the boys and girls of the press lit up meaningfully as they heard the word friend.

It happens often enough. The renowned Signor So-and-so is taken ill at a concert or in the opera house. Mr Never-heard-of-him steps up on to the platform and more than capably fills his shoes. A recording career will beckon at some point... But that's that's not going to happen in time for the morning papers. So a bit of back-story is a godsend as a fill-in. I wondered a bit grimly how my friendship with Michele would be portrayed in the morning's news. But it wasn't a moment for being grim. It was the biggest day of my life to date. Well, I thought it was, though it was difficult to be sure. Since meeting Michele just over two weeks ago, every day had been big. Bigger than anything that had been before.

*

We were late getting home. We hardly slept, Michele and I. We just lay together, squeezing each other, as if to reassure ourselves that we, and all that had happened to us, was real. Yes, it had really happened for Michele, but a little bit for me as well. It was not just the abstract question of what the press might say about us in the morning. In the morning I would have to go back into Verona and rehearse.

There were two more performances of Rigoletto to go. Friday's (which by this time of the night meant today's) and Saturday's. The singer whom Michele had replaced was not expected to be fit to sing at either of them. Michele had agreed to cover him for the whole of those two shows.

That meant his spending most of Friday rehearsing the complete role. It was wonderful that he already knew all his notes and words – and everybody had remarked on the fact that he'd done what he did without 'carrying the book' – but he still needed to be coached in the moves. And no-one had heard him sing the Duke's bits of Acts One and Two. Not even me...

The rehearsal pianist wasn't going to be free that Friday morning. So I'd been asked if I'd step up and play for Michele's rehearsal myself. There would be a fee, of course. I'd said yes with alacrity, knowing that was what Michele would have expected from me, and was immediately terrified, though I tried not to let it show.

In bed, of course I admitted that to Michele.

'How do you think I feel, then?' he said. 'How do you think I felt this evening?' Only this evening. It was just two in the morning now but already the evening just gone felt a lifetime ago.'

'I know you were nervous,' I said. 'We could hear it for the first few seconds. But I held your candle very tightly for you, and hummed along under my breath the way you once did for me.'

'Chele hugged me very tightly at that point. 'I think I kind of knew you were doing all that...' Then he said, 'I also remembered that note my mother left for both of us under the pillow before we went to Vicenza for the audition. *Be frightened of nothing and all will go well.*' He quoted it to me in Italian. 'I suggest that tomorrow, I mean later today, you think of it as addressed to you.'

'To you and me both,' I   said.

'Chele said, 'To *us*.'

*

It had been as short a night in bed as Juliet's with Romeo. We were on the road at eight, driving back to Verona to do a day's work. A day that would end mid-afternoon for me with any luck, but which would extend, for Michele, till after darkness fell, and the Arena was patined with ten thousand candle-stars. A tight knot of apprehension gripped my stomach, and I knew without having to ask that, despite his mother's written assurance, the same went for Michele as well.

A piano in the open air. Wheeled out from somewhere into that vast un-protecting space. Although it was a nine-foot Steinway concert grand I found I felt quite sorry for it out there in that huge arena, and that helped me a little way towards overcoming my terror at what I was about to do.

Yes, I had busked my way through Act Three of this score two days ago. But only for Michele's ears, not for those of my future employer, the repetiteur, and her employer, Grippi, plus any other singers who might show up in the course of the day, wanting to hear Michele's voice working in harness with theirs. And I hadn't touched Acts One and Two.

Reading an orchestral score is unlike reading a piano piece, with one stave, one line of notes for each hand. There is a different line for every group of instruments. There may be up to ten in all. You have to take them all in at a glance, see where they are different and where they are the same, then try to play as many of the notes you've glanced at as you can encompass with a mere ten fingers. You have to try to tell all the different stories the different instruments are telling, while making of it a coherent whole. Now do you see why I was terrified?

Yet once we started, my fear fell from me like a cloak. I was simply too busy to be scared. And a repetiteur is not so-called for nothing. I had plenty of opportunities to get things right.

I didn't even think about the newspapers till we stopped for mid-morning coffee. But then they were brought out to us. I knew we wouldn't have been shown them if there had been terrible things about us in them, so already, even before we looked at them, there was that relief.

There were pictures of the two of us, and some of Michele on his own. We both looked a bit startled. And in the ones where we appeared together we looked, at least in the eyes of anyone who was remotely wondering, like two young men in love.

Without exception the papers praised Michele's courage, his stage presence, and his voice. I won't go on at length. It was all good. When it came to me – as in all the stories it did – I was described quite simply as Michele's friend, who had joined in the rescue of Signor Grippi, and who had now landed a job as rehearsal pianist with Vicenza Opera. There was no innuendo, no suggestive winks or nudges. Readers could see the word friend and make of it what they wished. I was grateful for that.

The rescue, however, was described in very dramatic terms. The boat had grown in size, and it was with a massive and courageous effort that we'd all swum with it back to the shore. That the distance involved was a mere three metres, that the water was only chest-deep and we'd had our feet on the bottom all the way did not rate a mention. You were allowed to imagine the distances as having been much greater, and that we had dived into the water from something approaching the height of a cliff, rather than a seven-foot harbour wall. Sometimes the press can be good to you.

After coffee Michele had a costume fitting. These things can go either way. It's quite easy, though a bit time-consuming, to make a costume smaller. It's quite a different matter if the thing must be enlarged.

To everyone's relief it became apparent as soon as Michele got dressed – under the sky but in the relative privacy of a corner of the wings – that the singer he was replacing was the same height as Michele was, that he had the same length of arm and leg, and took the same size shoes. The only difference lay in their waist measurements. The difference was of about twelve inches. Michele, I'm happy to say, was the slimmer of the two. This discrepancy was noted with politely simulated surprise by the wardrobe staff – though, knowing the other singer as they did, they would have realised in advance. It was a problem easily solved, though. Jacket and breeches went away to be given some temporary tucks.

It wasn't till midday that either of us thought to ask – and it was Michele who did – 'I wonder what Sandro and Valentino are doing today.'

It goes without saying that the Luccinis had cancelled their younger son's English lessons for the day It was the elder brother who needed me most just then.

When I'd unthinkingly asked Sandro the same question in relation to Michele and Valentino a few days earlier, when we'd been on a boat together, sitting hand in hand, Sandro had answered, 'Much the same as us, probably.' That answer was hardly possible this time round. Whatever they might be doing it would certainly not involve rehearsing opera for a public performance and trying on Renaissance clothes. 'I really can't imagine,' I said.

We didn't eat much at lunchtime. It had got very hot rehearsing out in the open in the sunshine, even though the stage management had put awnings up as soon as they'd arrived at half past nine. Despite our many repetitions we had at least got through to the end of the opera by midday. (The Duke of Mantua does not appear in every scene, thank God.) Then, during the short afternoon session, the other lead singers appeared, to go briefly through the scenes in which they sang with Michele. This was the point at which I'd expected to feel most nervous, but I was over that by now. I'd been blooded that morning, just as Michele had been last night. I might be playing a humbler part in things, but I too was a professional now.

We were free by three o'clock. We could have driven home and come back again in time for the evening show. We didn't. We walked down to the edge of the River Adige, found a shady place there, lay down in it, and sank at once into the light, silvered sleep of outdoors.

We awoke a little before six, thanks to our presence of mind in setting the alarms on both our phones. I could have eaten like a wolf, but Michele didn't want to. A full stomach pressing upwards on the diaphragm reduces a singer's lung power noticeably, and the body's efforts to digest it slow the brain. So we compromised. We had a slice of pizza each (to be honest, Michele had one slice and I had two) a peach each, and some lemonade. We promised each other we'd stuff ourselves with pasta after the show.

A text came from Sandro. The four of them – Valentino and he, and the Luccini parents – were on their way in to see the entire show. They'd booked seats on the high stone tiers. Michele texted back that they must make sure to get cushions. The hardness of the stone seating would be crucifying if endured for the length of an entire opera.

Then it was time for Michele and me to part. He was due backstage and in his dressing room for the costume and make-up call. I walked around the pink streets for a little, alone for the first time in several days, and found myself in a kind of haze of wonder at what had happened to me in that short time. It seemed unreal. Yet it was so.

I had been given a ticket for one of the stone seats as a thank you for stepping in that day. That was in addition to my fee. So when the time came I made my way into the Arena and climbed, following the ushers' signals, to my allocated spot. They gave me cushions. And a candle for later. I said at that point, 'Could I possibly have two?'

I hadn't had a chance to find or meet up with the Luccini party. No doubt we'd all find each other after the end of the show. But at the end of the first act I caught sight of them, quite unexpectedly in all that crowd, about six rows lower down, in front of me. Act Two was about to start then, so I didn't rush down to say hallo to them. I would do that at the end of Act

Two.

Michele seemed to sing even better than the day before. There was no repeat of even that momentary failure of assurance of yesterday night. His voice ascended the giant steps towards me like a big invisible bird. And when he was singing his presence filled the stage. He looked stunning in his costume too, I thought. But then I was the one who thought he looked stunning whatever he wore. As well as in the nude...

The sun went down, and the sky went briefly gold. The stage lighting stole softly into play. One by one the candles around me began to twinkle. I looked down towards where the Luccinis sat to see if they were lighting theirs. I was just in time to see them do exactly that. Then I lit my two. I mean, 'Chele's and mine.

And when I'd done that, I looked back down at my... What should I call them? My friends? My second family? My in-laws? At the Luccinis at any rate. And I saw something else then. I saw Sandro's bare arm creep round the back of Valentino's neck. And a moment later I saw Valentino, a bit more diffidently, a bit more slowly, place his arm around Sandro.

NINETEEN

I was woken – we were woken – by a tap at the door. Then the door was opened before either of us could say anything or even collect our thoughts.

The brilliant light of mid-morning was streaming in through the curtains from over the lake. It was half-past ten. I'd slept too deeply to wake and return to my own bedroom as I always did before dawn. Michele and I, in shared horror, bobbed up into a sitting position in the bed, our two naked chests on show. (Why do people always do this, when burrowing down under the bedclothes would be a much more sensible choice?) Entering the room now was Sandro, wearing nothing except a pair of shorts, and carrying a tray.

'Momma thought you might want something to eat and some coffee,' he said, putting the tray down on the bedside locker, then going over to open the curtains like someone playing a butler in a film.

I inspected the tray's cargo. There was a pot of coffee and two cups. Glasses of fruit juice. Four croissants in a little pile. Two small dishes of strawberries and two plastic pots of plain yoghurt. It was a big tray. I said in wonder, 'And she put it all on the same tray? And asked you to bring it here?'

'It surprised me a bit too,' said Sandro nonchalantly. 'But yes.'

Michele and I exchanged glances, and I felt his bare hip rub mine.

Sandro said to Michele, 'You're the most brilliant

bloody brother anyone ever had.' Then he sort of pounced onto the bed, in the way that a much younger boy might, and jumped on top of his brother, cuddling him, naked chest to naked chest, and covering his face with kisses, the way I had no doubt he must have done when he was a child.

And then he sprang sideways onto me and, without asking his brother's permission or mine, with equal abandon cuddled and kissed me in the same way.

I didn't believe there was a heaven. But if there was, it couldn't be better than this.

After a moment or two he sprang back off the bed. 'We're off out in a minute,' he said. 'Valentino and I. We'll probably be gone by the time you get downstairs. So see you later, and have a good day.' He paused for a moment. 'We'll probably see you before this evening. But in case we don't... Oh, what is the expression you told me, Hen?'

'Break a leg,' I said.

*

It was Saturday. Michele had a performance to give in the evening. Until then he was free. There was no rehearsing to be done, either by him or me. Nor was Sandro going to have an English lesson from me today.

'Chele and I took the small boat out into the middle of the lake, took our clothes off and, despite the glare of the late morning sun, pretended we were in a gondola again. We were aware of the possibility of getting spotted by people in speedboats that came close. As we were now people who'd had their picture in the national press together in a professional context, a photo of us pleasuring each other orally in a boat would have been quite a scoop. But we were feeling a bit invincible this morning and felt we could handle that sort of exposure easily. In the event no boat came that close to us, no paparazzi helicopters buzzed overhead, no photos were taken. We were actually, a bit perversely, disappointed by that. But it was good to be reminded that we were still just two small people, and pretty unimportant, as anybody comes to realise, out in an open boat, naked, on that vast lake.

On the other hand, we were *us*.

Michele let me drive him to Verona at the end of the afternoon. That I would accompany him to Verona and attend his final performance there – final for the moment anyway – was accepted by both his parents as a matter of course. I bought myself a cheap seat at the very top of the stone tiers, and watched and listened to Michele, adoringly, like a dog. Even up there, right at the back, I heard his every word, his every bell-like note.

I took two candles again, when I was offered one, and when the time came, lit and held them both. I knew that he knew I'd be doing that. I knew that he couldn't pick them out among those thousands. And yet I knew he would.

On Sunday we all went to Mass together, at the little church by the stream, where the fish waved in the clear water under the bridge. A few people who had seen our pictures in the papers and who knew the Luccinis slightly came up to us and spoke. But that was all. We ate a peaceful lunch at the Piccolo, and lazed the afternoon away on the lakeside beach. Me and

Michele, Sandro and Valentino. There was no sign that Valentino was planning to go back home just yet.

It was Monday when everything kicked off suddenly. The phone began to ring at eight, and from then on it rang non-stop. Did Michele require an agent? At least a dozen people called to ask that. 'No,' I said. 'He has an agent. You're speaking to him.'

Of course he would need a real agent eventually. But we'd want to talk to a few people first. Including Signor Grippi. We didn't have to wait long for that. Signor Grippi phoned to speak to us. I mean, he phoned to speak to Michele. No, I did mean that. He spoke to *us*.

Grippi offered Michele roles in every production that was lined up for the autumn tour. He would be starting on the same date as I would be, in a few weeks' time, in rehearsal in Vicenza. We'd be working together from the first morning, in harness together from the very first minute of our very first full-time jobs.

In the meantime, and afterwards – Grippi said – Michele was welcome to accept offers of work from other sources, provided he cleared them with Grippi first. Was that acceptable? Michele looked at me for guidance. I gave him an agent-like nod.

Two magazines phoned to ask if they could run interviews with 'Chele. I said yes to those, plucking the first number I thought of out of the air and asking for that as a fee. I don't know if it was too high or too low, but they both said yes to it.

I called Grippi to ask about that. He thought the amount I'd asked for was not unreasonable, but suggested that for the future I should up it by about ten percent.

A wealthy man who lived nearby called. Or rather his secretary did. Did Michele sing Lieder by any chance? And would he be available to entertain a gathering of rather important people in the music industry at his house the following week? I said yes to all of that. Did Michele by any chance have a regular accompanist? Very regular, I said, and quoted a fee for both of us.

Again, Sandro's English course was put on hold. It could easily be extended by a few days at the end. And Sandro didn't seem to mind too much. He went sailing that day with Valentino in the yacht.

When things got quieter a few days later – and how perversely let-down we all felt when they did – it was back to teaching Sandro again. Not that I minded that. Nor did he. Nor did Michele. Nor even Valentino, who every day came along with us.

One evening, as we all sat outside the Loggia della Losa in the dusk, the people at the next table asked Michele for his autograph.

*

When the weekend came again, we decided to give each other a bit of a break. By this I mean that Sandro and Valentino decided to give Michele and me some time to ourselves, and Michele and I allowed Sandro and Valentino some time together without the encumbrance of us. It was agreed that it was Michele's and my turn to go for a sail on Saturday in the yacht.

We decided we would sail to the Punta San Vigilio first, tie up in the tiny harbour and enjoy a beer or something there, at the scene of our spectacular jump into the water and Michele's triumphant pre-audition rendering of La donna è mobile, draped in a towel. Then we would cross the lake and have a bite of lunch at either Gardone or Salò, depending on how time went, before sailing back home.

The yacht had been set up so that one person could sail her. All the controls that handled the sails were in reach – just about – of the person at the helm. Though you had to be quite agile. But it was fun to share the small workload between two or three of you, and I'd learned a lot in the last few weeks.

I looked back with amusement at my first attempts to steer. Sitting crouched on the plank seat, tight as a limpet screwed to a rock, holding the wheel with a vice-like grip as I over-steered, not waiting for the boat to respond to my commands in its own good time, first right, then left. These days I stood tall behind the wheel, my feet comfortably positioned on the cockpit deck, unconsciously bending at knees, waist and ankles as I adjusted my centre of gravity according to the movement of the boat. Letting the wheel run through my fingers until stopping it with a light touch.

We took it in turns that morning, trimming the sails and steering the yacht. Tacking a little because of the wind direction, we ran alongside the shore path that we'd walked along so many times. Past the Luccini's house – yes, we could see the gate in the wall between the bushes – then past the place where we'd had our first fuck, and where Sandro had caught us with our trousers – and everything else – off.

Seeing the Luccini's house caused me to ask a very obvious question, though it was one neither of us had broached till now. ''Chele,' I said – I was at the helm, he seated just beside me – 'where are we going to live?'

'I don't know,' he answered. 'I really haven't thought about it. Everything's been so quick. We could live at home, I suppose...' Even as he said it there was doubt in his voice.

'I know,' I said. 'The long drive to Vicenza every day. Staying sober every evening for the late drive back...' I didn't have the cheek to suggest that Emilio might take us the sixty miles there in the morning and bring us home at night.

'I suppose we'll have to get an apartment in Vicenza,' Michele said practically. I thought of the lovely house we'd just sailed past. Thought how I'd miss its spacious rooms, Fazioli piano, terraced gardens, its access to the lake, the boats... 'Of course we'd be back here at weekends,' Michele said. My mood brightened at that thought.

We rounded the tip of the Punta, entered the little harbour and tied up, being extra careful not to capsize the yacht... The waiters recognized us when they came to take our order. They not only remembered the 'rescue' and Michele's impromptu singing, but had read about our subsequent adventures, and Michele's moment of triumph in Verona, in the press. They wouldn't accept payment for our two beers but insisted we had them on the house.

There is a story by Mark Twain called The Million Pound Bank-Note. In it, a pauper who picks this unlikely piece of paper money from a gutter finds himself unable to pay for anything he buys in shops and eating-houses, because no-one can give him the change for the only currency he has. But his creditworthiness is taken for granted. Everywhere goods and services are given to him freely, lavishly, and he is treated with the greatest deference and respect.

It felt like that now for us.

We hoisted sail again and set out across the lake. Here, where the wind cut down from the northern reach there was a bit of a swell, or what passes for a swell on an inland water about twenty miles long by eight in width. We made good time, and went up the inlet that leads to the town of Salò, one of the few sizeable places on the lake that I hadn't visited yet. A Venetian town in days gone by, it achieved some notoriety as the last seat of Mussolini's government at the end of the Second World War, just before the Allies closed in – most of Italy now among them – and finished him off. That notwithstanding, it was a pleasant, handsome town to stroll in. I won't bother to tell you what we had for lunch...

It was late afternoon by the time we sailed out again. Before doing so Michele phoned Sandro. He told him where we were and about our planned route back. Sandro was back at home now, so 'Chele asked him to pass on the message that we weren't sure how long the return would take us. If we weren't back by cocktail time they weren't to wait for us for dinner. We'd get something in Garda when we landed there, before coming back. Was Sandro having a good day, by the way? Michele didn't add – *with Valentino*. Anyway, Sandro, without mentioning Valentino either, said that he was.

We left the inlet behind us and headed into the wider water of the lake. We came quite close to the empty island with the ruined house on it, whose Sleeping-Beauty otherworldliness I'd admired from the deck of the Verona on that first journey with the two brothers to Gardone, weeks before..

A double plume of spray appeared on the horizon ahead of us. It was the bow-wave of either a hydrofoil, we guessed, or a speedboat. As it drew nearer we could see that it was a speedboat. It was drawing nearer at a great rate, though, and we realised that its course was bringing it directly towards us. It was not our job to sail out of its way (anyway, which way? Left or right?); it was the responsibility of its helmsman or helmswoman to take a detour around our yacht.

'Bloody hell,' I said, 'they're leaving it very late.'

They were leaving it so late that we began to worry about them. Was it possible they hadn't seen us? Or were they doing it to scare us, with a childish prank? There wasn't time to try to contact them by radio. There was an electric-powered horn among the yacht's array of gadgets. Michele blew that instead. I'd never heard it in action before. It made one hell of a noise.

And then I realised. 'Oh fucking hell!' I said, or rather shouted. Michele had spotted the problem at the same moment, and swore in Italian very loudly, urgently. The problem was, there was no-one aboard the oncoming boat.

Michele was steering then. He pulled hard on the wheel and we began to turn slowly left. But there wasn't time to start the engine, let alone sail our way out of harm's way. I was hardly aware of the speedboat hitting us, broadside on, and carving us in half. I hardly heard the noise, the crashing, splashing, splintering. I hardly saw it happen. Hardly felt the huge impact.

I heard a great silence only. I felt the cold heaviness of the water around me, pushing me both down, it seemed, and up. I saw the darkness of the water below me. I saw the lightness of the water above. I found myself scrambling like a dog in the water, clawing myself up.

I broke the surface, choking and coughing, terrified because I couldn't catch my breath. I thought, I'm dying, and then, where is Michele? I'd never wanted him so very much.

I felt him bob beside me. I heard his voice. 'Relax. You're wearing a life-jacket. That'll keep you up. Just cough. But, sorry, we don't have a boat.'

I spluttered and choked. I spoke my first words a half minute later. 'I'm terrified,' I said.

'We just have to swim to the island,' he answered. 'We're only just off the shore.'

My head was so low in the water I couldn't see any sign of the island myself. 'It's miles away,' I spluttered – or was I snivelling? 'We'll never make it. I mean, I never will.'

'Of course you will, *stupido*.' I heard the sound of his little, loving laugh.

And then I felt his big hand under my tummy, supporting me, like a father teaching his boy to swim.

Then moment by moment I felt myself more in control of things. Michele was teaching me how to swim for myself.

'Towards, towards,' I heard him say. Together we began to make progress towards the shore.

TWENTY

At last I could feel the bottom with my feet. We waded up out of the water and arrived on a stony little strip of beach.

Everyone has some idea of what happens in Robinson Crusoe, whether or not they've read the book. Well, this was the Robinson Crusoe moment of my life to date. Though I had one advantage Crusoe didn't. He had to wait a long time before he found a friend on his island. I had arrived with mine already alongside me. Alive and intact.

In addition to our life-jackets we had shirts on, now wringing wet, of course. Incredibly, we were still wearing our deck shoes. We had also retained our sopping cargo shorts.

There is an episode in Robinson Crusoe in which he goes off swimming, to explore a part of the island cut off from him by a wall of rock. He removes his breeches to do this, swimming in the buff. Yet when he arrives around the corner and has explored a bit he munches ship's biscuits which he's had the forethought to put in his pockets... Critics regard this as a rather funny lapse on Defoe's part, which a bit of careful editing could have put right.

Well, Crusoe was a character in fiction, so it hardly matters. What we had in our pockets was: a phone each, a wallet each, with bank-notes all soaking wet, and a few coins. Thank heaven for button-pocket cargo shorts. I don't know if eighteenth-century breeches pockets would have fastened with a button or not.

On the other hand, we didn't have a biscuit between us. Not so much as a Mars bar or Kit Kat.

You try and phone, don't you? Even when you know there's no signal for miles around you. So we both did. With predictable results.

The next thing seemed to be to move inland. To reach the island's highest point. That would give us a purpose, at least, while we thought about what in heaven's name we were going to do next.

When you land on an island by boat there's usually a landing stage and a well-trodden way inland. Or at the very least you can choose your landing place, find a promising spot on an accessible beach. Arriving out of the water after a shipwreck you have no such choice. We were surrounded by thick scrub and bramble that came down to within a yard or two of the water's edge. We walked a short way in each direction but the vegetation didn't thin out. Yet we'd seen a ruined house from the water, and abandoned gardens that had looked, with the enchantment lent by distance, a bit like paradise.

So we pushed our way into the thicket. It would have been uncomfortable even with sturdy clothes on. In our flimsy, soaking wet apparel it was very much worse. Brambles tugged at our sleeves and tangled in our hair. The long sharp thorns of sloe bushes ran through our shirts and stabbed our chests. Our bare shins didn't escape either. There were nettles at just the right height to make sure of that. On the other hand, we were not worried about running into warlike native tribes. It was good to have one thing not to worry about.

Our doggedness was rewarded. After some twenty

yards – though it felt like ten times that – the scrub began to thin and we found ourselves in a tree and shrub dotted field of waving summer grass. Yellow and purple vetches flowered amongst it. There were bright stars of red campion too. Yellow rose of Sharon, St John's wort.

Some of the trees were cypresses. We realised we were in an old garden. This was what the sloping cypress-studded terraced lawns of the Luccinis' home would revert to if nobody ever cut the grass.

Big old fruit trees were laden with small apples. We were in July still. They wouldn't be ready for another month. We made an attempt on one or two though, even so, but soon gave up. The trees were full of climbing roses and clematis that had gone un-pruned for years. Their big blooms, mauve, pink and golden, peered down at us from among the branches, and sunned themselves on the leafy cushions of the tree tops.

We went on in a roughly uphill direction. After a while parts of the house became visible between the trees, and then we arrived at it. It looked like a nineteenth century building, with high, pointed gables and steep roofs made of slate. We seemed to be on the kitchen side of the building. A door stood slightly open. We pushed at it. It opened further. We went inside.

Had this been a fairytale we would have found ourselves in an opulently furnished mansion, with kitchen cupboards stocked with food. A place where time had stood still for years. But we weren't in a fairy tale. Whoever had abandoned the place, whenever that was, had removed every stick of furniture before doing so, and capped off the water pipes.

Time had not stood still here. It had peeled paper from the walls with fingers of damp. People had camped in here and left their rubbish behind them. They'd put graffiti on the walls, which 'Chele translated for my benefit.

Yet some things had survived. The ceilings had been painted with trompe-l'oeuil staircases to heaven, with cherubs gazing down at us between the banisters. We found the main hall at the front of the house, where there were real stairs. Very gingerly we started to climb them, expecting at any second to find our feet disappearing through a rotten tread. We felt an Everest-like sense of achievement when we stood together at the top.

Here were bedrooms aplenty, though no beds. We had to content ourselves with the views from the windows instead. Which were to die for. We looked out over the apple trees below us, over the roses and clematis that climbed them and now looked up at us. Over and between the cypresses at Garda Lake. How placid and friendly it looked from here, all blue and sparkling. It seemed impossible to think that such a gentle giant as Lake Garda had swallowed our boat.

There was the Punta San Vigilio five miles across the water, and the bay of Garda village, basking in the late sun beyond that. From the other side of the house we could look back to the nearer shore, towards Gardone and Salò. The nearest point was still more than a mile away by the look of it. Would Michele shortly ask me to take my courage in both hands and swim with him across that? I shrank from that thought.

He did say something at that moment, though it wasn't that. He put an arm around my shoulder as we leant on that windowsill looking out. He said, 'Isn't it time I had a kiss?'

So we hugged and held each other, standing at the open window, pressing up against each other's still wet clothes. Our lips and tongues found each other's and our shrunk dicks groped for each other's company through two pairs of damp shorts. And for a minute or more it no longer seemed important that we'd got ourselves, far from food and running water, into this terrible fix.

'We need to signal,' I said. Michele had taken the lead in everything from the moment the boat sank. I thought it was time I took the initiative for a bit.

Michele agreed that signalling our presence here was a priority but asked, what with? We could build a bonfire in the garden easily enough, create smoke while daylight lasted, then a pillar of flame in the dark. But what would we light the fire with? We had no matches on us. We started to search the house.

Other possibilities...? We had no torch. The electricity was off. So find a flat piece of soil and lay out curved rows of stones there, that would read SOS?

It's often the case that when you go looking for something you end up finding something else. We failed to turn up matches, but unearthed in one of the cupboards four cans of fizzy orange drink. We both gave a spontaneous whoop of thanks. You'll wonder what we found to open the cans with... They were ring-pulls, thank God. We didn't open them yet, though. They were the most serious of our possessions at this moment. We'd wait till we were really thirsty, and even then space them out. If we had to spend the night here...

We went outside again. There was still an hour or so before the sun set, but we needed to think quickly about what needed doing before it got dark. In the gardens, looking for flat open ground to lay stones on, we had another piece of luck. We found ourselves in a kitchen garden, very overgrown, but full of half hidden fruit. Among the weeds were raspberries and strawberries and mouth-puckering redcurrants. There was rhubarb growing in tall clumps. And there was a cherry tree, jewelled darkly with luscious fruit. We wouldn't starve, at least. And fruit is mainly composed of water anyway. It would help eke out the precious fizzy orange cans, when it came to dealing with our thirst.

We stuffed our mouths with berries and cherries. We bit off chunks from the crunchy rhubarb stalks. It's a really great thing to do if you have a dish of sugar handy to dip the sticks in. It's a bit sharp on the palate if you don't.

We broke off from our meal to look for stones, and a place to lay them out. We found the latter quite by chance. There was a concrete floor that had belonged to an outhouse now demolished, about twenty by thirty feet. The stones were another matter, though. We hadn't really thought about how many we'd need if we were going to write letters big enough to be read from the air. How long it would take to assemble them. We'd barely got as far as the first quarter of the first S by the time half an hour had passed. By this time the sun had disappeared behind the trees, flashing intermittently between the branches as it prepared to leave us for the night.

We gave up on our SOS. We couldn't finish it before sunset. Tomorrow we'd have the whole day in which to finish it. We'd have the whole rest of our life...

We returned to the kitchen garden. We stuffed ourselves full of strawberries and raspberries again, and munched more cherries and rhubarb. Rhubarb can be quite filling if you can manage to eat enough of it. We did our best.

The plan was then to go indoors, take a can of fizzy drink upstairs with us and drink it before lying down and trying to sleep until first light.

What a heavenly thing, a things of unimaginable delight, a can of fizzy orange is. It is the nectar of the gods. Until this moment neither of us had realised that.

We couldn't sleep, of course. We wanted each other like crazy by now but the bare dusty floorboards of a decaying bedroom were not at all conducive to sex. For the moment anyway, as dusk turned to night outside the window, we sat propped up against the bedroom wall, knees drawn up to our chests, arms around each other's shoulders – at least our shirts were dry by now – and talked.

'You hardly ever speak about your parents,' Michele said at one point. 'Though you have mine rammed down your throat the whole time.' We both laughed as he realised what he'd said. 'I mean my parents.'

I said I knew he meant that. 'Mine are fine with me,' I said. 'They know I'm gay. I can't pretend the knowledge positively delights them, but they want me to be happy, and that's that.' They'd also been fine when I'd phoned to tell them about the rehearsal pianist's job. 'They're happy about my staying on in Italy,' I went on. 'I'm the Sandro of my family. They've got an heir in the form of my elder brother. I'm the spare. It's not the end of their world if I live six hundred miles from them.' Nor was it the end of mine.

I reached down between Michele's hunched-up thighs and his chest and tried to feel his cock through his shorts. Michele accommodatingly shifted his knees a bit so I could manage this. He said, 'I know you'd had a bit more sexual experience than I'd had before we met. But – before us, I mean – had you ever been in love?'

I thought hard for a second. 'No,' I said. I added, 'Of course, you have.'

'Yes,' he said. 'I fell heavily for some of my school-friends, though it didn't work the other way around. Then Valentino, of course. I fell for him, and he for me, though he never admitted it to himself or to me until last week.'

'Bit of a waste,' I said.

'Not really,' said Michele. 'When you think how things have worked out. In a way it's like getting a flame from a cigarette lighter out in the open. Sometimes you need several goes at it before you get a flame that lasts.'

I said, 'Though in my case I got the lasting flame the first time round. My first and only experience of falling in love has been the only one I want.'

I thought then of the phrase: love hurts. I hadn't understood it properly till I met 'Chele. Being with him was so wonderful that it was painful. It was painful, in a way, to be with him now. As for being without him, even for a few hours, that was a kind of torture, I'd discovered. I'd discovered something else about this strangely exquisite torture. The more you loved, and the more deeply you fell into each other, and the better it got for the two of you ... the more it bloody hurt.

I noticed something strange about the window above us in the opposite wall. Although the sun had gone down less than an hour earlier, the sky seemed to be getting light. Surely we hadn't fallen asleep while talking, and it was now dawn?

I pointed the phenomenon out to 'Chele. He said, 'I think perhaps the moon is rising. Shall we go and look?'

We got up, a bit awkwardly: our legs and arms were stiff. We walked to the window and looked out. There was a certain brightness in the sky, but we were looking west. We walked out and across the landing, into a room that gave onto the east. And there, behind the distant low snout of the Punta San Vigilio, a three-quarters moon was coming up. Unsticking itself from the distant mountains. It made the black land below it even blacker by contrast, but it threw a long net of silver out to us across the deep lake. A long causeway of a net which lay trembling and shimmering in front of us. It ran all the way between us and seven-mile distant Garda village. We could have walked home along it, jumping from strand to strand among the silver mesh. Just for a moment, before it rose from its earthly anchorage, we could have walked all the way to the moon.

I said the first thing that came into my head. 'Do you

want to go outside?'

The air was fresh and soft out there. It was a warm night. The lights of all the lakeside villages encircled us like broken necklaces that we glimpsed between the trees. As we walked, our moon shadows followed us, gambolling like porpoises in our wake – or more like squirrels actually, as sometimes they ran quite fast up the trees.

We found a place in the apple orchard where the grass was not too long and not too thick with bristly things, and then we trampled it with our shoes. Just in case of snakes or scorpions. We weren't afraid of moles or mice.

Then we kicked our shoes off. Slowly removed our shirts and shorts. The moonlight made Renaissance statues of us though, unlike most of those, we two had hard, standing dicks. We stood looking at each other in wonder. So did our cocks. As we moved in towards each other, so did they. They met before we did and the tips of them kissed each other lightly just before our lips embraced.

Michele knelt down and engulfed me. 'Don't,' I said. 'I want you to fuck me, 'Chele,' I heard myself saying next. I hadn't known till then that I wanted that. Nor had I expected myself to voice the thought so loudly. But I didn't want to come in advance. Anyway, for once there was no-one to overhear us within miles.

He drew me down onto the patch of hay meadow we'd flattened. I let him arrange me the way he wanted me. Playing passive at this moment, I let him handle me as a child plays with a doll. He placed me on my back and anointed himself with saliva. Then he lifted my legs with the crooks of his arms. I felt his tender probings and then his triumphal entry into me. He pushed himself into me gently and we looked earnestly face into face. Then he lay slowly forward, his warm chest on mine. I looked into 'Chele's eyes, thinking, this wonderful being is mine. For better or worse. And I was humbly his.

He smiled back into my eyes, though with a slightly quizzical look. 'What a predicament we're in,' he said. 'And yet,' marvelling at the thought, 'we still want this.'

'That's because we're us,' I said.

'I love you,' he said.

It took him a long time, this time. I can't say I minded that. When he was nearly ready to come he took my cock into his hand and rubbed it quickly and fondly back and forth. A moment later his thrusts into me grew strong and urgent. I felt him swell inside me and burst. And a moment after that my cock followed the example of 'Chele's, and I fountained on my chest. And then we lay there naked, Michele's cock still inside me. It was only a short time, I'm pretty sure, before we were fast asleep.

TWENTY-ONE

I woke up, cold and cramping, wondering where I was. I tried to turn over but found I couldn't do that without turning Michele over too. My effort woke him of course. He said, 'Has my cock spent all night inside you?'

I said, 'I think it has.'

He pulled it out at that point and wiped it with a bunch of grass. We reached around us for our clothes. Shirts and shorts only, but they were better than nothing, at this time of night. Whatever time of night it was.

The moon was in the middle of the sky, so we'd clearly slept for a few hours. I said, 'I could murder another can of fizzy orange.'

Michele said, 'What happens when we finish it?'

I said, 'We've got a whole lake to drink.'

We went back indoors and shared a can of the nectar of the gods. The lake could wait its turn. We might yet be rescued before the fizzy orange ran its course. Then we lay down on the floor of the bedroom we'd sat in earlier, and went into a dozing kind of sleep.

A thrush woke me. It seemed to be repeating and repeating an Italian phrase I didn't understand. That was while I was still half asleep: before I realised what it was. The pale gold light of morning was filling the window now. By the time the sun had risen properly we were out in the garden again. We shared the third can of fizzy orange. That left us just one more. We gulped down some handfuls of strawberries, then cherries. We competed to see how far we could spit the stones from our mouths.

And then we had to start collecting real stones again – like unfortunates in a Greek myth, I thought – and painstakingly assembling them into the first giant letter S. Flights into Valerio Catullo airport hadn't begun this early. No-one would be looking down on us yet. But the sooner we got cracking the better for us. An SOS that was written in stones might be spotted even from a landing passenger plane. Something resembling a small letter c – that was all we'd achieved so far – would ring alarm bells for no-one at all.

The service boats would start up around nine o'clock. We thought that at that time one of us could go down to the shore and try waving and shouting to them while the other went on slowly, like someone knitting a jumper, creating the first letter S. It would make sense for the shouter and waver to be Michele, we agreed. He had the louder voice. He spoke Italian, and if necessary could belt an operatic aria out over the water in an attempt to make himself heard.

But before we had time to put this plan into effect we heard the sound of the motor of an approaching boat. We peered between tree trunks to see if we could see it. Soon we did. It was a patrol boat belonging to the lake police.

We ran down through the gardens and orchards, then struggled more slowly through the belt of thorn and scrub that ringed the island just above the beach. At last we were down at the water's edge. The boat was not far off shore at that moment. We waved crazily towards it, but evidently no-one saw us, since it began to turn away from us, heading towards Salò. 'Sing something,' I called to Michele urgently. Then at that moment I saw two figures on the boat that I recognised. They were Sandro and Valentino. I said, 'Ilkley Moor!'

And so we began an emergency rendition of it, at full volume. Michele's voice sailing effortlessly out across the water, mine full of raucous urgency.

'Where as ta been since I saw thee,

Since I saw thee?

On I-ilk-le-ey Mo-or bah-aht a-at...'

And we hardly dared to believe it when, a few seconds later, the nose of the police launch began to turn slowly in our direction and then to make its bobbing way towards us.

*

The story came together piece by piece. Michele had told Sandro we might not be back for dinner, so nobody was alarmed when we didn't show up. At bedtime eyebrows were raised because we still weren't back, but still nobody was alarmed. We were two grown men who'd gone out for the day, after all, and it wasn't even midnight yet. Everyone simply went to bed.

It was only this morning early, when Signora Luccini got up and listened to the local radio news that she became worried. The news announced the disappearance of a speedboat. Someone at Sirmione had hired one and, not knowing quite enough about handling the thing, had started it up and set the throttle, having just untied it. Its rapid acceleration had thrown him out. He'd been pulled out of the water at once: he was right beside the quay. But nobody had been able to catch the boat. It had headed out into deep water, heading north west and had then disappeared from sight. By the time anyone thought to track it on radar there was no sign of it anywhere...

Signora Luccini had gone to our bedroom and, without knocking, walked in. Our bed was empty of course. She went immediately to wake Sandro ... but found his bed empty too. Valentino's room next. She'd been relieved more than anything else to find her younger son there, curled up asleep with his new friend.

Those two had thrown clothes on – once they'd rung our phones and got no answer – more quickly than they'd have believed possible before. They raced Valentino's car down to the harbour to see if the yacht was in. When they found it wasn't, they called the lake police, and were soon heading out with them towards Salò.

'We wondered whether to land at the island first and look for signs of you, or to go on to Salò. We'd just decided to go to Salò first and try the island later if we'd found no trace of you when we heard you singing.'

'It was a very strange song,' said one of the police officers who were with us. 'It didn't sound like an English song – or an Italian one.'

'It comes from Yorkshire,' I said. 'Which is something different yet again.'

'Perhaps it was a good choice, then,' said the policeman, poker-faced. 'Had you sung something

Italian – something from opera, maybe... Rigoletto or something like that... Well, I mean, you could have been just anybody, and we'd have gone on past.'

I drew myself up to say something like, 'Do you know who we are?' But then I saw the policeman give Michele a broad wink. He had probably known him since Michele was a kid.

*

'Your brother saved my life,' I told Sandro later. 'It's as simple as that.'

'It isn't that simple,' Michele said. 'If Hen hadn't been with me in the water, needing me, loving me, giving me all of himself... If his head hadn't popped up in the water beside me, I think I might have given up. Slipped under again and drowned. Life-jacket or no life-jacket. I'm not a strong swimmer...'

'You are,' I said. 'You powered your way through the water with your legs and just one arm. You were supporting me with your other one.'

Michele looked at me strangely. 'I was?'

'Don't you remember?' I said.

'I remember your hand under me, Hen, bearing me up,' Michele said.

'You remember what?' I couldn't quite believe I'd heard that. I saw Sandro and Valentino exchange a glance. I had a sensation then of something very deep, deeper than the deepest depths of the lake. Something deeper, though more wonderful, than I would ever understand.

Anthony McDonald

VALETE

Valentino and Sandro are still together, one year on. When Sandro went off to study English in Rome last autumn Valentino applied to do a post-graduate degree in the same place. There wasn't a spare place left in his main subject, which was economics, so he's doing a course in English literature instead. He said at first that it wouldn't have mattered if the course had been nuclear physics. He was only doing it so that he could be in Rome and with Sandro. But now he's actually loving it, and we discuss the books he's studying whenever we meet.

They have a fine apartment on the Palatine Hill, which overlooks the Farnese Gardens. The gardens bring a welcome breath of air to the place in summer, while in winter the apartment is very snug. Something that Sandro didn't know till he moved in with him is that Valentino is a brilliant cook.

As for Michele and me, we have a house of our own, with a garden, just outside Vicenza, on the bank of the River Bacchiglione, which looks dreadful written down on paper but is in reality full of charm. The mortgage repayments are a bit eye-watering, but then so are some of the fees Michele gets. And with my more modest but at least dependable salary as a rehearsal pianist to add to the pot, we do more than just get by.

It was strange, last autumn, to find ourselves starting our new jobs together, on the same morning. We had butterflies in our tummies, both of us. It was like a first day at school. It was strange to be working together, though we had different jobs to do, in the same rehearsal room. Me struggling with the orchestral score of Carmen, 'Chele learning the role of Don José. And then we got used to it. It became like working together at the piano in the Luccini's lakeside house. Our workplace became an extension of our home. It just happened that there were a few other people there.

You won't remember me telling you that we'd been booked, just before our boating accident, to give a recital of German songs in a rich man's house, which a number of people in the music industry would attend. Well, that went ahead, not many days afterwards. It was a spectacular success. Michele sang the whole of the Schöne Müllerin cycle. I had to make a conscious effort not to spoil things, as I played the accompaniments at the piano, by humming or joining in.

The audience didn't exactly go wild. People in the music industry tend not to do that. But they did better things. They showed their appreciation by offering us jobs. Michele got a recording contract that would take him to sing Schubert in Rome. There was a recital earlier this year in London. There's talk of New York next year...

It hadn't hurt us, the fact that our boating adventure got us back in the national press again. Our pictures had appeared together for the second time. We were billed as partners this time round, and readers could decide for themselves what they wanted that to mean. It was wonderfully convenient for the press that someone they'd given inches of space to after he'd taken over the role of the Duke of Mantua that night in Verona should find himself just one week later involved in a spectacular yachting accident in which he nearly drowned. I got the feeling they hoped he'd do something similar again one day soon. He and his 'cute boyfriend'. (Those words were Michele's at the time, not mine. But I can't help quoting him verbatim. I'm only human.)

Now, with Vicenza Opera, we've been on tour. We've played Venice. We did Padua... It was a very special moment for Michele. To find himself singing as a professional, and as a hot ticket, in the city where he'd appeared as an amateur and an operatic hopeful in his student days.

We've been further a-field than that this year. La Scala in Milan. Paris and Madrid. We haven't got as far as Covent Garden in London yet, or the Metropolitan in New York. Those things are coming, though, Grippi assures us. That's fine with us. You can't do everything all at once and, anyway, who wants all their treats in the same week?

Now we're having an early summer break. We haven't gone far away. Just as far as Michele's parents' house at Garda. They're away this fortnight, and Emilio and the secretary-cum-cook are on holiday too. So we have the run of the place, just the two of us. Michele's quite a good cook also, by the way, about which I'm pleased. It wouldn't matter if he wasn't though. I'd love him just the same.

We're spending our time here quietly. Days out yachting on the lake. Yes, there's a new yacht. Hats off to the Ancient Greeks, or was it the Phoenicians?, for inventing insurance claims.

In the evenings, if 'Chele isn't cooking at home, we dine on the village lake-front at the Piccolo. We watch the sun go down from there, or from the terrace of the Loggia della Losa just a few doors away. And sometimes we have a nightcap in the little piano bar in the tunnel behind the square.

This evening we haven't bothered with the car. We walked down through the gardens and through the little gate in the wall onto the lakeside path. We held hands some of the way. If people see us we don't care. Take pictures of us on their phones and hawk them round the press? We'd shrug. That's life. And we're just us.

The roses on the lakeside are even better this year than last, though I can't help feeling that the jasmine that climbs the wall on the landward side of the path has not flowered quite so heavily this July. Michele said I was imagining that. At least it's just as fragrant, I had to agree.

Now we've had our nightcap and are walking back home through the dark. There's just enough light to not need a torch. Just as we come to the limit of the throw of the pillar lamp behind us the one ahead of us comes to our rescue around a corner in the nick of time.

Michele has one hand in the pocket of my shorts. It's a habit of his. I like it. I always feel his hand belongs there. As does mine in his. I've just put it there now. In a few minutes we shall be at the garden gate. We may choose to close it behind us when we go in, then play naked on the lawn like kids under the stars. Or we may decide to row the boat out into the lake a little way – along the moon's gleaming causeway if there is one tonight – and pretend we're in a gondola again.

Either way we shall end up making love together. One

way or another we always do. On the lake or in the garden? The decision is a small one. The big decision is the one we've already made. Or not made... It may be that our intentions played little part in what has happened to the pair of us. It doesn't even matter which way we make love tonight. 'Chele inside me, me inside him. Or in his mouth, or he in mine, or me in his hand quite simply, and he in mine. It doesn't really matter even whether we have sex tonight at all. We have the biggest thing already anyway. It's called love. Its other name is ... *us*.

THE END

****

Anthony McDonald is the author of over twenty novels. He studied modern history at Durham University, then worked briefly as a musical instrument maker and as a farmhand before moving into the theatre, where he has worked in every capacity except director and electrician. He has also spent several years teaching English in Paris and London. He now lives in rural East Sussex.

Novels by Anthony McDonald
SILVER CITY

THE DOG IN THE CHAPEL

TOM & CHRISTOPHER AND THEIR KIND

RALPH: DIARY OF A GAY TEEN

IVOR'S GHOSTS

ADAM

BLUE SKY ADAM

GETTING ORLANDO

ORANGE BITTER, ORANGE SWEET

ALONG THE STARS

WOODCOCK FLIGHT

MATCHES IN THE DARK: 13 Tales of Gay Men

(Short story collection)

Anthony McDonald

Gay Romance Series:

Sweet Nineteen

Gay Romance on Garda

Gay Romance in Majorca

The Paris Novel

Cocker and I

Cam Cox

The Van Gogh Window

Gay Romance in Tartan

Tibidabo

Spring Sonata

Touching Fifty

Romance on the Orient Express

All titles are available as Kindle ebooks and as paperbacks from Amazon.

www.anthonymcdonald.co.uk

21929001R00122

Printed in Great Britain
by Amazon